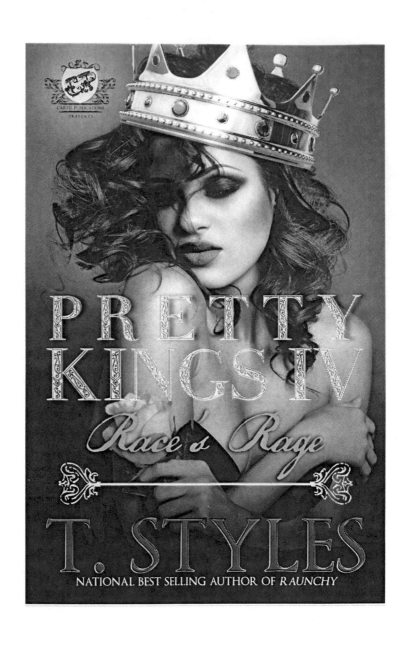

CARTEL PUBLICATIONS
PRESENTS

PRETTY KINGS IV

Race's Rage

T. STYLES

NATIONAL BEST SELLING AUTHOR OF *RAUNCHY*

Are You On Our Email List?

Sign Up On Our Website

www.thecartelpublications.com

Or Text The Word:

Cartelbooks To 22828

For Prizes, Contests, Etc.

4   **Pretty Kings 4:** Race's Rage

WWW.THECARTELPUBLICATIONS.COM

By **T. Styles**   5

PRETTY KINGS 4

RACE'S RAGE

By

T. STYLES

Library of Congress Control Number: 2016958175

ISBN 10: 1945240024

ISBN 13: 978-1945240027

Cover Design: Davida Baldwin
www.oddballdsgn.com

www.thecartelpublications.com
First Edition
Printed in the United States of America

By **T. Styles**   7

What's Up Fam,

First I want to say THANK YOU all for continuing to rock with us for over 8 years and now, 65 books! It feels great having a loyal fan base that we can continue to bring our best to. And we will keep bringing it! Ride with us, you won't be disappointed!

Make sure you check out both our Web Series', **"The Worst of Us"** and **"It'll Cost You"**, that are currently available on YouTube, DVD and Amazon Instant Video for download. Also, Season 2 of, "The Worst of Us" airs on November 15th on YouTube. We hope you enjoy them much as we did making them!

Without further delay we bring you, "Pretty Kings 4"! Lawd Have Mercy!!! It's SOOOOOOO much going on in this book that my mouth stayed open man! I mean, T did an AMAZING job of weaving these characters together and I swear I didn't see most of the drama coming. Trust me, you will love this one. For me, outside of the original one of course, it ranks as the best of the series so far! Get ready!

With that being said, keeping in line with tradition, we want to give respect to a vet or trailblazer paving the way. In this novel, we would like to recognize:

Les Brown

Leslie Calvin "Les" Brown is a motivational speaker, an author and a former politician. His words and videos are so powerful and moving, I often wake up and put him on before getting out of bed. Les focus is on getting people to reach their full potential in life and accomplishing their dreams! He speaks from experience as he has made everything he set out to do or have come into existence. If you need an extra push to motivate you in any way, check out the words of Mr. Les Brown and get ready to be inspired! You can see his videos on YouTube.

Aight, get to it. I'll catch you in the next novel.

Be Easy!

Charisse "C. Wash" Washington
Vice President
The Cartel Publications
www.thecartelpublications.com
www.facebook.com/publishercwash
Instagram: publishercwash
www.twitter.com/cartelbooks
www.facebook.com/cartelpublications
Follow us on Instagram: Cartelpublications
#CartelPublications
#UrbanFiction
#LesBrown
#PrayForCeCe

CARTEL URBAN CINEMA'S 2nd WEB SERIES

IT'LL COST YOU (Twisted Tales Season One)

NOW AVAILABLE:
YOUTUBE / STREAMING / DVD

www.youtube.com/user/tstyles74

www.cartelurbancinema.com

www.thecartelpublications.com

Pretty Kings 4: Race's Rage

CARTEL URBAN CINEMA'S 1st WEB SERIES

THE WORST OF US (Season One)

NOW AVAILABLE:
YOUTUBE / STREAMING/ DVD

www.youtube.com/user/tstyles74

www.cartelurbancinema.com

www.thecartelpublications.com

Season 2 Premieres November 15th on YouTube

By **T. Styles**   11

CARTEL URBAN CINEMA'S 1st MOVIE

PITBULLS IN A SKIRT – THE MOVIE

www.cartelurbancinema.com **and**

www.amazon.com

www.thecartelpublications.com

#PrettyKings4

By **T. Styles**   13

Evil is a thirsty entity that needs a human vessel to survive. It will take refuge in a hateful heart, a failing relationship or a broken family.

Never invite it in.

Even in the name of revenge.

- T. Styles

PROLOGUE

PRESENT

The soft overhead light glistened against the elaborate table settings around the perimeter of the wedding hall. Just one silver fork alone was worth enough to pay a hood nigga's rent for a month. And yet it was just one of the many finishing touches in place for Abd Al-Qadir's descendent, who was marrying his new bride via an arranged marriage within an hour.

The ceremony had yet to take place but everyone who was anyone in Saudi Arabia was invited to the mystical celebration in a small suburb of Washington D.C.

All were happy.

Arabic music played quietly in the room and was intermixed with popular American tunes, as Jawad was a fan of the culture.

Finally it was time.

The door opened and Abd, Jawad and his groomsmen walked to the front of the hall and awaited the arrival of his bride. Mixing the Middle East with the West, the audience was in awe at the multi-million dollar ceremony unfolding before their eyes.

The celebration was moving art.

A spectacle to behold if that's what you were in to.

Jawad was handsome but Abd was striking. Standing over six feet tall, he possessed rugged good looks that appealed to women of all nationalities. The hairy beard that connected to the lower half of his face was coal black and resembled a mink coat.

Dressed in a white suit and a red and white Keffiyeh, Abd strolled over to his son and placed a firm hand on his shoulder. From a far he noticed that Jawad was jittery and feared he would walk away from his destiny, as he threatened to many times before. "Don't worry, she'll make you happy, Jawad," Abd said as he looked down at his son, before smiling in a fake manner at the crowd. He was doing his best to calm the suspicions of the guests whom he was certain noticed his son's anxious mood.

The man looked as if he wanted to be anywhere but in that bitch, locking his life with someone he barely knew.

Jawad smiled although it only lasted for a moment. "I know, father. She's beautiful and—"

"Our family needs this marriage to go off without a hitch," Abd said harshly. "You know Rana's father is powerful in Saudi and here in America as well. With their support we can do many things, son. Do not destroy this for our family because you are unwilling to do your part and make her your wife." His voice grew deeper. "It will be a grave mistake."

He nodded. "I understand father," he whispered. "And I don't mean to sound ungrateful. Maybe it's the nervousness you detect and I will do my best to rid myself of this weak emotion at once."

Abd placed a firmer hand on his shoulder. "Good. You are my son and we are never fearful about a future we control. Don't worry; even as your wife you will have many women but also many heirs." He pointed at him. "The choice will always be yours unless it conflicts with mine."

Jawad shook his head. "Yes, father. And again, I will pull myself together."

Just then the music grew louder as everyone in the room rose to show respect to Jawad's veil covered wife. A small smile spread across Abd's face as he looked at her henna decorated hands holding an elaborate bouquet of colorful roses speckled with gold, red and white.

Standing in the wrong place, Abd walked away and reclaimed his position as Jawad's best man and waited as the others did for the ceremony. This wedding would net the once over billionaire more money than he could spend and he needed it to go through seamlessly.

But something was wrong.

Where was Rana's father who was supposed to walk her down the aisle?

Why was she coming to enter the next phase of her life alone?

His question was answered when suddenly the bride lifted her veil and Abd was gut punched when he realized he was staring into the eyes of Bambi Kennedy. It was a takeover of an amazing kind. Something he had not prepared for.

Speckled in several other positions Bambi's crew rose with powerful assault weapons aimed at Abd and his guests. "I am Bambi Kennedy," she announced, as she dropped the bouquet that was used for nothing more than a cover for her weapon. "And I am here to right the wrongs that have occurred to me." Her focused moved toward Abd who was throwing her looks that could kill. "Sadly enough, most of you will die tonight. So I suggest you say your prayers."

CHAPTER ONE

SOME WEEKS EARLIER

BAMBI KENNEDY

Tension was high in the Kennedy compound. We were sitting around the long black roundtable at our home and everyone was screaming at the top of their lungs. With voices so loud my temples pumped with throbbing pain. We called ourselves trying to come up with a plan to deal with the recent threat Abd Al-Quadir had thrown our way after promising to kill us unless we produced Mitch, the plug I assassinated to take over his business.

But our meeting was a bust.

No one was seeing eye-to-eye and all I wanted was a drink to clear my mind. A bottle of vodka would've gotten me right if I'm being honest. But Kevin was playing me so close that my desire would have to remain a wish.

For now anyway.

To make matters worse Abd had called several times to hold a meeting with me and I ignored all of his requests. I valued my life and being face to face with death did nothing for my purpose. Besides, I dumped Mitch's corpse a long time ago and there wasn't shit else to talk about.

So I refused hold council with Abd, even realizing it was a huge mistake.

"All I'm saying is that everyone should be keeping a low profile," I said standing up looking at Race, Denim, Scarlett, Bradley, Ramirez and Kevin. I rubbed my long black cascading hair out of my face and stuffed my hands into my green fatigue pants. "Unless it's an emergency, we don't need to be cruising the streets when—"

"I'm not putting myself through this shit again!" Bradley yelled stabbing a stiff finger into the table. "I can't even visit my brother's grave because once again we gotta hide on account of you." He pointed at me, eyes dark with hate. "I'm sick of this shit!"

"On account of me?" I yelled, my brows lowering. "Nigga, I'm the reason the business kept going after you and your brothers decided to stay in hiding a few years back. Oh, but you don't want to talk about that shit because it hits home right?"

A while ago Kevin, Ramirez, Bradley and Camp popped up in a white van in front of our other house after we moved on with our lives due to believing they were all killed at the same time. It turned out that when the mass murderer came into the casino they were in, our men thought The Russians were trying to attack them by masquerading behind the killer. So while the bodies were dropping they were able to escape but instead of telling us they were alive and in hiding, they stayed away.

Even though we were worried sick.

It was me who rounded up the girls and ran the drug operation and I deserved my respect.

"We'll give you your points on keeping the business floating or whatever, but you're also the one who killed Mitch!" Bradley yelled. "And there wasn't any reason to because he did right by us on the price. We all know it."

"Don't be delusional! Mitch was gonna cut us off, Bradley. Remember? We kept him locked upstairs in that attic for months." I pointed to the ceiling. "I needed to make sure I did whatever necessary to keep the bricks coming in including killing him."

Bradley thinks he's slick.

I know why he really hates me.

He tried to kill me a little while ago believing that I was going to tell Denim that he fucked Grainger, her sister.

But I got back at his ass too.

It was midnight when I sought my revenge. The nigga was in the shower and I could see the steam flowing from under the door. With Race at my side I waited patiently for him even though he took forever to wash like a bitch. Taking a whole thirty minutes. The moment he opened the bathroom door and crossed the threshold, I knocked him in the head with the butt of my gun while Race pointed her chopper at his dick.

Forcing him to open his jaw, I made him suck on my barrel before knocking him upside his head again. Once I had his full attention I let it be known that if he ever put his hands on me again I would murder him, brother-in-law or not. Despite the beef I never told Kevin knowing full well he would assassinate his own brother if he knew what Bradley did to me.

If the Kennedy's were good for anything it was keeping secrets and I was no different.

"You still made a decision without clearing it with us," Ramirez said.

I wiped my hair out of my face again. "If we let Mitch live he was gonna—"

"He was gonna what?" Bradley yelled standing up. "You don't know what the fuck he was gonna do because you killed him without approval so shut the fuck up with all of that noise."

Kevin, who sat next to me rose to his feet. "I love you, Bradley, you my brother but if you disrespect my wife again I might shift your jaw upwards."

Denim touched Bradley's hand. "Baby, please..."

"You know what, fuck all of this. I'm gonna do what I want to anyway. Ain't no need in arguing with you niggas." He stormed out the meeting.

Something happened to him when he went to prison recently for raping Grainger but he wouldn't tell us what. It definitely impacted his mood that's for sure.

Kevin remained standing next to me. "I hate to admit it just as much as you all do but we are in another crisis. In order to get out of it we will have to keep a low profile because we don't know what Abd is capable of."

"We've heard his legend," Denim sighed. "And I think the part that's troubling Bradley is that we can't stay in this house forever. We have to live our lives even if we are being stalked."

Kevin took a deep breath probably because the meeting was going nowhere. "And I'm not saying you can't live your lives, just be careful. Is that too much to ask? We already lost Camp and...and...my son. I don't want to lose another member of this family."

Several months passed and I was still finding it difficult to admit that my son Noah was gone. Due to a hit the Russians orchestrated. It was so bad that I didn't want Melo to go back to college but he begged, as we doubled down on security to ensure he stayed safe.

Upon hearing Kevin's words Ramirez held his head down.

I took a seat and seconds later felt Kevin's firm hand on my shoulder. "Look, we at war," Kevin continued. "There's no two ways to say it and I don't think neither Bambi or I should have to repeat ourselves." He took a deep breath. "Now what does that mean? It means that since the world won't stop revolving while we survive yet another attempt on our lives, we have to move with extra security everywhere we go. Or stay in this house until it's clear."

I looked up at Race, Scarlett and Denim who were staring directly at me waiting on my word. They wanted to know what I felt. It was as if Kevin was in charge of the men and me the girls. I realized I looked weak but after losing my son I didn't have the strength these days to move the way I used to.

Who could be strong after losing a child?

Even one who hated me.

If we were gonna make it this time I would need their help.

Race shrugged. "I'm not gonna hold the cross and complain about it. I mean...we dope dealers and I guess this comes with the territory."

I looked at Denim. "You already know I'm gonna do what's necessary, Bambi." She stood up. "But let me go check on my husband. He's pretty upset about it all." Denim walked away.

My eyes then fell on Scarlett. "Ya'll know I'm not much of a fighter. But I'll continue to do my part by manning the Dope Phone. I just want us to remember we picking up Master today, which raises an additional concern we have to worry about."

"Things will be fine," Kevin said pointing at her. "Trust me."

"I understand and I want to believe you. But maybe we shouldn't get him now," Scarlett continued. "I mean...maybe we should let him stay with the Reverend until—"

"That boy is a Kennedy and my brother's son." Kevin yelled speaking a bit louder. "And I want him home where he belongs."

Scarlett nodded but it was obvious she didn't want Master here and with her past I wasn't sure if now was a good idea either. At the end of the day Scarlett lost her daughter because she was a child abuser, what's to say she wouldn't do the same to Master? I mean, I had all intentions on keeping an eye on her and my nephew but I wasn't moving the same.

I didn't feel the same.

About life.

Ramirez sighed. "Brother, you know my motto. No guns formed against the Kennedy's shall prosper. Whatever you need me to do I'll do." He tapped Race on the shoulder and they both exited the meeting, leaving us alone.

Now it was silent.

Kevin reduced his height by sitting next to me, letting out an exasperated breath. With a firm but gentle hand he rubbed my back before raising my chin so that our eyes met. "You being too hard on yourself."

"Kevin..."

"Listen to me. I love my family and you know I would die for each one of the niggas in this house. But we can't put the weight of their existence on our shoulders."

"At the same time this family can't handle any more loss," I whispered.

He nodded. "We will handle whatever comes our way. We are Kennedy's and so we do what we must."

I sighed. "Why does everything seem to be happening at once?"

"Who are you?"

I frowned. "What?"

"I asked what's your fucking name!"

I sat up straight, thinking he was going crazy with this split personality shit. One minute he was consoling me and the next he was flipping. "Bambi. Bambi Kennedy."

"Remember that shit. Because the next time you play weak in front of the family I might have to rethink that ring on your finger." He stood up and stomped away.

RACE KENNEDY

Ramirez was sitting on our bed, staring in my direction and he's getting on my fucking nerves. I'm like give me five seconds alone...PLEASE!

When I looked over at him I noticed he kept rubbing his hands on his jeans like they were moist. Which is something he always did when he wanted his dick sucked.

Boy, bye.

Lately he tried too hard to get us back to where we used to be and I was starting to resent giving our marriage another chance. When I said I would try I thought we would talk about the past minimally. To be honest I preferred to take it slow, make love and try to become friends again.

But he was playing me too close, wanting things to be the way they used to be when I was young and dumb. It wasn't happening.

I didn't feel like talking to him about if I still thought about how he went outside of the threesome arrangement we made with Carey, to see her without me. Or that he got her pregnant. I killed the bitch even though I cared about her and it was time to move on.

In my mind she was no longer relevant.

How could she be?

She was dead.

His consistent persistence and pushing the relationship to be as it was before his deceit was the main reason I met someone new. Well, not necessarily met but it felt good to have someone to talk too outside of the Kennedy Klan. A bitch could talk about drugs and paper for so long before her pussy dried up.

Unaffiliated with dope, my new friend provided relief and an escape and I enjoyed him for it.

I was standing in front of the mirror in my bedroom, when I grabbed one of the wet wipes to clean the makeup off my face. When I turned around Ramirez was naked, rubbing his stiff black dick and staring at me like a perv. "Come over here and kiss it for me."

I knew it. He was trying to fuck.

And I wanted to throw up.

Back in the day when he wanted to get freaky I would drop everything to fulfill his desire but that was pre Race Kennedy, the drug boss. I was no longer naive and lately it seemed like everything he did was a turn off.

I grabbed his navy blue Polo velvet robe off the back of the chair and threw it in his face. "Cover yourself. You look like a whore."

He stabbed his arms through each hole of the robe, rushed up to me and grabbed my medium length hair, yanking it hard. I smiled despite the pain and feeling the anger steaming off his skin. "I know we got our problems but I'm not about to let you disrespect me, Race. Get that shit outta your head right now."

I looked up at him.

"Get...the...fuck...off...me...Ramirez."

Slowly he released his death grip. "I'm sick of this shit. I need to know if you want to be with me or not!" He pointed at the floor. "I'm not gonna keep apologizing for some shit I did back in '72."

I giggled in his face. "I know you don't got your years that fucked up."

"You know what I mean. It was a long time ago. Let the past float away."

"So what you doing now, Ramirez?" I rubbed my throbbing scalp. "Threatening to find another whore? If so have at it."

"I don't want anybody else, Race. The only woman for me is you."

"Then why you keep acting like you doing me a favor by being with me?" I paused. "Huh? Every time you don't get your way you do this shit and I'm tired of it, Ramirez. I'm tired of feeling like if I don't perform in the right way you'll go to your second in pussy command. This is me. Either get use to it or cut me off. Your choice and if the truth is present I don't give a fuck no more."

I wiped the rest of my makeup off and he stared at me the entire time through the mirror with disdain. If I didn't know him well enough I would assume he was contemplating killing me. When my phone rang I smiled when I saw it was a text message from my 'New Friend'.

Grabbing it I said, "I gotta take this." I made a move for the door and he blocked me with his hating ass.

His arms crossed tightly in front of him, robe hanging open he said, "Let me see what's on that phone." He pointed at it.

I grinned. "Do you really want me to pull your phone out and start going through shit?" He stepped out of my way. "I thought so."

I walked to the second floor bathroom, sat on the edge of the tub and texted my friend back:

TEXT MESSAGE

ME: Sorry so late. Was held up.

NEW FRIEND: It's okay. You're worth waiting on.

I smiled and he didn't say anything real yet.

The creepiest part is I hadn't even met this man in person and already I was cheesing. How we came about was actually strange. I was doing some FX makeup for a client on an indie project a few months back, during the Mitch era. The movie was about the street life and two brothers who made a decision to date the same woman because she was perfect to both of them. On the makeup set that day there was only the director, who was handsome, two actors, who were also attractive and the wardrobe guy who was gay.

So I knew it couldn't be him.

After leaving the set I wasn't even in my car for five minutes before I received a text message from a number that was unknown. My New Friend said he wanted to say something to me on set but he realized I was married. And that the coward part of him wanted to say something anyway but was too afraid of being shut down. Still, the man in him couldn't let me walk away forever without at least trying.

And I was intrigued.

I'm in an unfulfilled marriage and being a major drug dealer means leading an isolated life. So if this person wanted to be a part of my world than I was willing to take a chance. I didn't even ask whether he was the director or one of the actors because it didn't matter. I queried him on some facts that occurred on set to be sure he was really there and he had me.

I wanted adventure and had no intention on taking it further than text. At least that's what I told myself.

He was like a digital pen pal.

My little secret.

TEXT MESSAGE

ME: You always know what to say to me.

There was a very long row of silence and I felt alone again. Suddenly my expression lightened when he responded.

TEXT MESSAGE

New Friend: One day soon we have to meet again. I need to feel you in my arms. That is...if it's okay with you.

I took a few moments to respond. I know Ramirez and I went outside of our marriage to fuck a bitch or two but we were always in agreement. Ramirez was the one who took it a step further by seeing Carey, without me, and falling in love. But if I agreed to meet my New Friend I would be an adulterer too and I wasn't sure if I wanted to take such a major step in the opposite direction. My betrayal could mean the end of our marriage and I knew I loved Ramirez.

Just didn't like him very much at the moment.

Everything was on the line.

Especially my peace of mind.

My thumbs grazed over the warm screen of my phone and finally I typed my answer.

TEXT MESSAGE

ME: I'm ready whenever you are. Just say the word.

CHAPTER TWO

SCARLETT KENNEDY

I had the phone pressed against my ear as I sat on the comfortable black couch in my room.

I don't know what made me stay in the lair we created for Mitch upstairs in the attic and field the calls for dope drops. Not just for the DMV (DC, Maryland & Virginia) but also for around the world. Maybe it was because it was luxurious, private and quaint. No matter my reason my desire to stay in the piece of heaven in the compound meant I had to take some serious responsibilities. With Sarge's help since he had been working directly with Mitch before Bambi took him out, the operation ran smoothly.

And it needed to continue to run smoothly for me to justify my existence. I was Sarge's support system.

Besides, the world thought Mitch was still alive and this was necessary because the cocaine plant he built in Mexico would only work for him. One sign of mutiny or Mitch's death and the manufacturers would probably take the operation from us. Luckily Sarge built a bond with Mitch prior to his death that included talking to our manufactures and facilitating distribution around the world. Things went on without a hitch.

"Yes, we have it and the fresh fruit will be delivered to your restaurant tonight." I sat back in the plush recliner, closed my eyes and took a deep breath. This secretary shit was the pits. "No problem, sir."

Of course we weren't delivering fresh fruit or talking to sirs. I was chatting with dope dealers and killers. But you couldn't necessarily say cocaine over the phone either. Even if the lines were what we considered untraceable or tap-proof.

I placed the phone down and when I opened my eyes Ramirez was standing in my room. I leapt up and looked out the door he just strolled through before moving back over to him. "What you doing up here?"

Unconsciously I rubbed the sides of my red hair that was pulled in a tight bun on top of my head, before gazing down and checking my True Religion blue jeans and black top for flaws.

"Just seeing about you." He smiled and I wished he'd stop. "No need in looking over yourself, you look perfect."

I tried not to smile because my beauty was the only real thing I had in this world. I paced the floor and placed my hands on the side of my head. "Ramirez, we can't—"

He moved closer and I inhaled his cologne. Damn he smelled good and I'm sure Race couldn't keep her hands off of him. "I just want to see how you doing, Scarlett. Ever since we made love you walk around the house ignoring me. Did I do something wrong? Didn't I make you feel good?" He reached for my hand and I pulled away.

"I'm your sister-in-law. We aren't supposed to be fucking. You know that so why the games?"

He smiled but it drifted away quickly. "In Roman times when the brother died the widow automatically went to the brother. Camp ain't here no more, the least I can do is take care of you by making you feel good. Can you let me do that without the games?"

I crossed my arms over my breasts. "Except you're forgetting one problem, you're married already."

He looked down on the floor. "It was a bad joke. Especially considering Camp died not too—"

"I can't have sex with you no more! I can't sleep with you knowing you belong to Race. Please don't try and make me. I'm begging you."

He laughed. "Actually I don't know if you can say that anymore. I'm talking about the me belonging to Race part."

He walked closer and I could feel my pressure rising and my clit thumping inside my black lace thong. What I wasn't sure about was why he turned me on the way he did. Maybe it was the danger, who knows? I never allowed myself enough time to think about what we did together when I was alone because my betrayal hurt too much.

To give us space I extended my hand. "That's close enough, Ramirez. And what do you mean about Race?"

"She doesn't want to be with me." He shrugged. "In that way."

"You expect me to believe that?"

"I expect you to hear the truth, Scarlett." He frowned. "And why do you seem afraid of me now?"

"You're dangerous. And you know it."

"I just want to be your friend, sexy." He grabbed my arm, pulled me closer and placed his nose into the pit of my neck. He might as well have kissed it or licked it because the feeling was the same.

Erotic.

"I just want to smell you..."

I sighed and shoved him. "Please stop!"

My push was weaker than I wanted but still I gave it a try. Finally I took a deep breath and completely separated my body from his. Trust me when I tell you it took a lot. More than I had in my soul.

"You are not to come back here again, Ramirez."

He flashed his smile. "You sure about that?"

"I'm positive. Why you ask that anyway?"

"Because you holding the cuff of my shirt."

I looked down at my hand, grasping the cotton and quickly let him go, before wiping my sweaty hands down my jeans. "Ramirez, do not come back here." I took a deep breath. "I'm serious."

"If I don't listen what will you do? Because I'm a Kennedy." His expression grew serious. "And a

Kennedy nigga always gets what he wants. You know that."

And then I saw something.

Oh no!

I frowned and looked over his shoulder. I felt like I had been gut punched at who was watching us, standing in the doorway. Ramirez turned around and joined me as we both focused on Bambi gazing in our direction. He cleared his throat, stepped further away from me before looking at Bambi. "I'm going to check on Race."

He walked out the room.

When he first came here I wanted him gone and suddenly I felt terribly alone. Like the other woman who'd been caught with a man who didn't belong to her. By a family member at that.

My marriage to Camp made me a Kennedy but we weren't together anymore, even before he died. In truth I was just an outsider trying to do my best to keep this family in my life.

To show my worth.

And I wanted nothing more than to remain a Kennedy.

My mind fluttered and I needed desperately to know how much she heard but was too afraid to ask.

So I just stood in front of her.

Waiting.

Possibly for her to tell me to get out like Camp had so many times when we failed to agree.

"You ready to get Master?" She asked in a low tone.

She was letting this go? She wasn't going to even question why he was in my room? My jaw hung but I quickly raised it again. "Uh...yes...when did you...wanna...?"

"Let's go now." She walked away.

She seemed cold.

Her response short.

But I definitely realized that she knew something.

The only question was how much.

CHAPTER THREE

BAMBI

"Where the hell is Scarlett?" Race asked me as we paced in the foyer of the living room. She was supposed to be here thirty minutes ago but she was missing in action. I was about to go get her when she walked downstairs, a look of guilt fresh on her face.

I had my ideas why she had this expression and for now I'll keep them to myself. I didn't know if Scarlett and Ramirez had anything going on. I walked in on the tail end of the conversation. But what I will say is this, something didn't feel or look right.

Finally she came into the foyer and I wondered why she changed her clothes. She was now wearing a white tank and white jeans that set off her red hair. Just like my other sister-friends, her beauty blew me away every time I saw her. "Sorry, guys, I got held up on a call."

"Well come on," I said grabbing my keys off the small glass table by the door. "Security is out front waiting and we have to still meet the developers for our apartment building in—"

"I'm not going," Scarlett said looking away from me. "I was just coming down here to let you both know."

Race focused on me and then her. "We not leaving that little boy over them people's house, Scarlett. You heard what Kevin said. We talked about this already so stop fucking around and let's bounce. The longer we wait the more we're going to lose daylight."

"No...I mean...I'm going to get my son...just alone."

I finally got it.

Something had happened between she and Ramirez and she didn't want to sit in the car with Race. She was probably blame worthy. If I find out that he seduced her I will kill him with my own hands.

That's on everything I fuck with!

Not only for sleeping with my sister but hurting my other one too.

I took a deep breath. "Scarlett, you shouldn't be doing anything by yourself. Now I know you're afraid of being a mother and you want some more time to think about this alone, but we need you to be safe and that means not cruising the streets unprotected."

She moved closer to us. "Just let me do this by myself, Bambi. Please."

Race shook her head. "Whatever, but that baby better be in this house tonight." Race pointed at her. "Because I don't know what your problem is but we don't leave our own in the world fending for themselves."

She's telling the truth.

Melo had already returned to school and although I wanted him home he wouldn't hear of it. Because of it we talked to the university and was allowed to have security around him at all times, even as he slept in his dorm room. Melo didn't want it that way but I was not losing another son.

Eventually he relented.

He had no choice if he wanted to go back to college.

"I'm going to get Master, Race. I just want to do it by myself. I hope you understand but I started this mess by giving them my baby and I want to clean it up."

Race shrugged. "Do what you gotta do. But if something happens to you I'm going to kill you." She giggled before walking up to Scarlett, kissing her on the cheek and looking into her eyes. "I love you, sis. Just want you to stay alive and safe out here. Okay?"

Scarlett smiled. "Got it, Race."

We walked out.

With the heightened threat on our lives, when we opened the door, there were two black vans in our oval shaped driveway filled with armed soldiers. One would tale behind us while the other would trail in front of us. Two of the men stepped out of the front van and helped Race and I inside of my black Cadillac Escalade.

Moments later with me behind the steering wheel I drove away, our entourage along for the ride. We weren't even halfway to our meeting before Race started texting someone and smiling.

I looked over at her and back at the road. "Ramirez got you grinning that hard? Must be good to have a marriage rekindled. I'm happy for you."

She cleared her throat and stuffed her phone into her pocket. "Nah, it's just a friend." She shrugged. "Nothing to be up in arms about."

I frowned. "Come on, Race. You don't have a friend on this planet I don't know about. So who was the person on the phone? Talk to me, I need an escape."

"First off I'm grown, second of all don't you think its unhealthy not to have an associate outside of this family?"

I frowned. "What's unhealthy about having us as your only comrades? The people who you can trust the most in the world because we know all of your secrets like you know ours?" I shook my head. "Besides, the last friend you had stabbed you in the back. You saw what going on the outside got you, nowhere. We all we got."

"Wow...a low blow. From a Kennedy friend at that." She shook her head in disgust.

I sighed. "I was wrong for my comment, Race. I just want you to be careful that's all. Everybody rolling around like this Abd mothafucka is not a sincere threat. The Russians may be gone but there are other killers out to get us in the world and they will do a good job if they find a weakness. I mean, how do you know this person you keeping time with is not part of the plan to take us out? You chose wrong with Carey and you may be choosing wrong with this person too."

"You don't think I know that, Bambi?" She yelled. "You don't think I regret the day I took Carey into our bedroom? Into our marriage? The last thing I need right now is you telling me something I think about daily."

Silence.

Something was going on mentally with Race and with the family being in heat I wasn't trying to argue with her. I wanted her to know if anything that I was on her side. "I'm sorry, Race. I'm an ex-military soldier and sometimes I push too hard for what I believe in."

She wiped her hand down her face and took a deep breath. "I apologize, too. It seems like everything happening with our family is bringing me down and—"

"Then lean on your husband. Not an outsider."

"Bambi..." She waved the air. "Drop it already!"

"I'm serious. You took him back, Race. Don't let him get away again because you not talking to him."

"Oh, so your marriage is perfect?"

"How you sound?" I looked at her and focused back on the road. "Kevin and I go up and down with our relationship like breaths. All he cares about now is me not getting drunk. But he's my husband and I'm in his corner. I'd kill a bitch if she got in the way of that."

She looked at me, longer than I could stand so I focused on the road again. Besides, I wasn't trying to give her my suspicions on Ramirez and Scarlett.

Not yet anyway.

"Somebody fuckin' with my husband, Bambi? Because if you know something you better not hold back. I wouldn't do it to you."

I sighed.

The problem was I didn't know anything concrete. I didn't see Scarlett fucking Ramirez. All I saw is the energy between them as he stood in front of her in that attic.

Maybe that was enough.

"Don't play with me. You know if somebody was coming at Ram I'd kill them first and tell you later."

She shook her head. "I'm tripping. I know you would."

I stopped at the light.

"All I'm saying is that if you love him maybe you should show him. Don't get me wrong, ain't none of them Kennedy's perfect but they belong to us until we say so anyway. So if you not calling it quits now you better protect what's yours."

"And like I said when it comes to Ramirez I have—"

Suddenly the mailbox on the corner exploded with a bomb blowing the van and our men in front of us in pieces. A large orange cloud with grey smoke veins spread out before our eyes. The impact alone made a ringing noise in my head that reminded me of the war in Iraq and suddenly I was filled with a mixture of emotions.

Quickly afterwards, the van behind us was fired into, killing all of our men.

"GET THE FUCK DOWN!" I yelled at Race as I saw the devastation.

I thought America was under attack, until from a car that sat far enough from the damage not to be impacted, Abd Al-Quadir came into view.

I'm standing in front of Abd Al-Quadir and the first thought that came to mind is crazy. He's more handsome than I envisioned and for some reason that makes him scarier.

"I'm sorry about the explosives," he said running his hand down his silky black beard, which looked wet like ink. "It's just that I needed to get your attention and you wouldn't take my calls."

I stepped closer. "You killed fifteen of my soldiers, Abd! How can you consider yourself a businessman and make moves like that? I could've been hurt! If you kill me you get no Mitch. You do know that right?"

"Come now, Mrs. Kennedy...you have more men." He said slyly. "That I'm sure of."

I froze and looked around the all white room where armed men dressed in black, red veils covering their faces as they held assault weapons trained on me. "What do you want? There has to be a reason for all of this."

"It's simple actually." He rubbed his hands together. "I need you to produce Mitch."

I frowned. This man was pissing me off. It wasn't like his dope was not moving as fluidly as it did before Mitch died, courtesy of us. If anything the circulation was better because we needed to put on fronts or people would've gotten suspicious. But he was being controlling, needing this done his way. "I told you Abd, that he doesn't want to be seen. So he's entrusted me to see to it that—"

I could see the veins of his temple pulsate. "You're use to talking down to men. Forcing them to lower their nature and do what you say, aren't you?"

"I never talk down to a man who deserved my respect."

He moved closer and walked around me before stopping in front of me again. I felt like I was on display and with the weapons trained on me he could do what he wanted with my body and that horrified me even more.

His stare was intense and he seemed to be looking through me. He grabbed a strand of my hair, sniffed it and released. "You know, in my country all women must have a male guardian. And within this law a woman is not able to marry, divorce, get educated or leave the country without our approval. Our laws help keep women like you in place." He pointed at me, his finger rested on the tip of my nose. "That's what America's missing. The authority of a real man."

I tried to walk away when he yanked my hand. "Get off of me!" I told him.

He smacked me so hard I tasted my own blood. "How you speak to men could have your hands cut off and stumped in my country. We may not be in Saudi but you will respect me as I stand before you." His teeth bore.

"You're going to pay for hitting me." My breaths were heavy. "I promise you."

He laughed. "And how do you plan on doing that? By getting your husband involved? I could kill everything you love with a wave of my finger." He laughed long and hard.

"So why don't you? Instead of doing all of this shit." I threatened although I wished I could take it back. He was more powerful in the moment than I was and we were in no position to go to war.

"Because I want Mitch." He paused. "And you have ten days to produce him. Not eleven. Not twelve. But ten."

"And if I don't?"

"Bambi, for your sake let's hope that question is never answered."

CHAPTER FOUR

DENIM KENNEDY

I was pacing in the grocery store by the fresh fruit when my mother finally walked inside, taking what seemed to be her sweet time. Like she wasn't supposed to be here an hour ago.

Fuck!

I agreed to meet her here, in private; because Bradley would divorce me if he knew after everything she put us through that I was still helping her out financially from time to time. But she was my mother and I couldn't turn my back on her if I wanted so I put it all on the line.

When he asked where I was going today instead of with the girls to get Master, I told him shopping. Unlike Kevin and Bambi he didn't feel like the threat Abd was throwing was as dangerous so as long as I promise to bring a van full of men to guard me he was cool with me leaving the compound.

But it was all a lie.

With my daughter and sister dead my mother was all I had and I needed to be there for her.

Maybe it was the mothering sense in me that had arisen making me want to nurture again.

Who knows?

I even tried to have another baby but Bradley had taken to barely touching me. It's like I repulsed him no matter how hard I tried. How could I have a kid when my husband wouldn't fuck me?

When I saw my mother walk in I stomped up to her and two of the armed men followed. "Ma, what took you so long to get here?" I noticed she gained more pounds, despite having the weight loss surgery and getting closer to her original size when she was a model. Her flesh pushed at the dirty grey sweatpants she was wearing and perspiration dampened the dingy white t-shirt she was draped in.

She looked nasty.

"I don't have a car, Denim so I got here as quickly as I could." She grabbed an apple off the rack and bit it.

She's messy as fuck out here.

"Ma, I gave you a brand new E Class last week and enough money for gas for six months. What happened to the vehicle? I know you didn't crash it."

She waived her hand and leaned against the watermelons, causing one of them to roll onto the floor. Talking with a mouthful of fruit she said, "If you must know I sold it, Denim. It was mine anyway. I was allowed to right?"

I stumbled backwards. "That car was beautiful! Fuck you sell it for? It was brand new!"

"For a place to stay!"

I moved closer. "Ma, I bought you that car and paid off your apartment lease for two years." I held up my fingers. "You not making sense out here." I dropped my hand. "What is going on with you?"

"The management company threw me out, Denim." She stood up straight and tossed the half eaten apple back on the pile. "If you must know the truth, there it is sitting in front of you. I was evicted of all things. They acting like they hurting somebody and shit."

"But why?"

"They claimed I was having too much company and bothering the neighbors. The truth is everybody in that high sadity building don't want nobody having fun with they old dry asses. So what I had a party or two. I was lucky to be done with them once and for all." She shrugged. "So I'm on the street now."

I sighed and rolled my eyes. "Ma, what are you doing to me? I can't keep giving you money only for you to throw it away. You have to be more responsible. Bradley gonna start noticing the cash I peel off our emergency stack at the rate you going."

"You know what, if you don't want to help me no more than that's okay. Although you might as well just say it." She turned around. "I'll just kill myself because I don't have anything to live for anyway."

My eyes widened upon hearing those words and I rushed up to my mother, walked in front of her and wrapped my arms around her as best I could. The musty odor of her body made my stomach churn and I figured she hadn't washed in days.

"Mother, please, listen to me." I released her. "You know I want to help, it's just that with everything I'm going through I can't deal right now with all of this extra-ness you got going on.

Money is not a problem but I need you to take better care, ma. I can't be out here in the streets because someone is trying to kill my family and me. If Bambi even knew I was out here she would lose it."

"Your family huh?" She tried to cross her large arms across her chest but it wouldn't work so they hung at her sides. "Listen at you. You carrying on as if Bambi pushed you out of her army pussy."

"You know what I mean."

She held her hand out and wiggled her fingers. "Do you have my money or not? I don't have time for the lecture and shit."

I shook my head and dug into my Louis Vuitton purse. I looked around before removing a stack worth seven thousand dollars and slapping it into her hand. She smiled and dropped it into the designer bag I bought her. "Thank you, baby girl. This gonna keep me right for a few weeks."

"What are you gonna do now, ma? Where you gonna go?"

She walked closer. "That's just it, Denim, I don't know." She shrugged. "Since Grainger died I'm out here for myself. I guess what I'm saying is

I need you. Have you ever stopped to think that I act out because we don't have our bond anymore? And I'm doing all I can to be closer?"

"You have me, ma. And I don't think you're acting out."

"Yes you do think I'm acting out." She rolled her eyes. "And it's okay. I just want us the way we use to be."

I sighed. "What does that mean? What do you need from me?"

Her eyes widened. "To live with you."

I backed up. "Ma, I...I can't do that."

"Why?" Her nostrils flared. "Because of your precious husband? Who would rather I die than be with you?"

"The last time you saw Bradley you fought. I don't even understand why you would want to live with us again. The drama would be worse than anything you can imagine."

"Living with you was the only time I felt at home. And I'm sure if you'd just try, you could convince Bradley and Bambi to let me back into the compound."

I shook my head slowly from left to right. "I don't know about this, ma. Not this time. Things got really bad the last time you were there."

"With you is the only place I belong." She took a deep breath. "Make it happen, Denim. Or don't be surprised if you hear about my body on the side of the road because I've taken my own life." She jiggled away.

Just then my phone rang. It was Race and she sounded frantic.

RACE

We were standing in the dining room trying to sort out everything that I witnessed before the Abd attack.

I was a nervous wreck but Kevin, Bradley and Ramirez were no better than I was. Everyone was nervous. I can't believe Abd went through so much to get his hands on Bambi. Blowing up mailboxes and having a firing squad assassinate our other soldiers was not only a crime but also a federal offense and he didn't give a fuck.

What am I talking about?

We kingpins!

All this shit's a federal offense.

"What exactly happened again?" Kevin said stomping up to me. Squeezing my arms. "Don't leave anything out."

"Aye, man," Ramirez said stepping in front of him. "Take your hands off her. She done told you ten times already how it went down. We all want Bambi back but you not about to hurt my wife to make it happen."

Kevin maintained his grip and stared at me crazily.

"Kevin, I know you worried about your wife but this is mine," Ramirez pointed at me. "Now I'm telling you to let her go."

Kevin looked down at me, blinked and released me. I rubbed my throbbing arms. "I'm sorry, Race," Kevin said in a low voice. "I just can't believe this mothafucka had the nerve to take my wife." He wiped the sweat that formed on his brow. "I mean, who does he think he is? I don't give a fuck how many niggas he got on the streets I'm about to wage war!"

"I know, Kevin," I sighed. "But Bambi is tough and she'll be okay. She dealt with these types of people in the army."

"If something happens to her," Kevin said through clenched teeth. "I can't take it, man. Not right now."

Just then Bambi fumbled through the door and Kevin rushed her.

We all did.

He lifted her off her feet and kissed her on the lips before taking her face between his hands as he stared into her eyes. "Baby, oh my God, you okay?" He took a deep breath. "I thought something happened to you. I thought he took you from me."

"I'm fine, Kevin," she kissed him back. "I promise you I'm shaken up but unharmed." She walked to a chair and flopped on it.

"We gotta get this mothafucka!" Kevin yelled pointing at the floor. "TONIGHT!"

"We don't know where he lives, Kevin!" Bambi yelled.

"Well where did he take you?" Bradley asked.

"I was blindfolded. After the explosion all I remember is the door being yanked open, me being pulled out and a burlap bag thrown over my head." She looked up at us. "The next thing I knew I was in an all white warehouse. No furniture. Just Arab men dressed in all black and red."

Ramirez paced. "This war shit going on far too long. We gotta do something."

"Well what did he say, Bambi?" Kevin asked.

"He wants us to produce Mitch in ten days. He says if we don't he will hurt people we love starting with dismantling our soldiers." She sighed. "I'm telling ya'll, after what I've seen with the bombs I know he can do it. We need to stay in this house until things blow over and we develop a plan. If what happened to me is not a good enough reason for us to stay in the compound I don't know what is."

Kevin sighed.

"This family needs a miracle," Ramirez said. "Like yesterday."

Just then the door opened and Scarlett walked inside. She was holding Master in her arms and he was smiling brightly. "Hey everyone, he's home," Scarlett said cheerfully.

CHAPTER FIVE

RACE

My girls and me were sitting in the hot tub in the poolroom talking about Abd and what his interference meant for our lifestyle. The threat was so great that I wanted to know if we were finally going to pay with our lives for our love of the dope game.

Maybe killing Mitch really went too far.

Bambi seemed tired but she was willing to give us five minutes to discuss how everything went down before going to bed. I wanted more details despite seeing that she was drained. Even before this she was dealing with losing Noah and with Melo back in school, heavily guarded of course, she was always on edge.

"He seemed so calm talking about what he was going to do to us if we don't produce Mitch," she sighed. "I think this threat may be the one to bring us down if we let it. I mean this nigga blew up a van!"

"I'm so sick of being on the run," I said as I ran my wet hand down my face. "Like when will it ever end?"

"Who knows, Race? We gonna have to lean on the fellas more than ever," Bambi said. "We can't do this one by ourselves."

"Speak for yourself," I said rolling my eyes. "Fuck my nigga."

"You still beefing with Ramirez?" she asked me.

"It's not about beef, it's about respect."

"Maybe you should let that go, Race," Bambi replied.

I frowned. "Wait, so I should just pretend like he didn't fall in love with that bitch, going against our agreement?"

"Why you keep acting like you weren't fucking her too?" Denim added. "Sounds like you doing the most when you have no room."

I was heated as fuck. I felt like I was being ganged up on when I should be feeling the opposite. They were my friends, not Ramirez's. "Yes, I fucked her too but like I said, we made some promises before our arrangement went down. And one of them was to not get her pregnant and more than anything don't fall in love. He did it all." I paused. "I'm not asking any of you to agree with my lifestyle but it's still mine. I don't point fingers at you bitches so don't judge me."

"You know what, I'm gonna go check on the baby," Denim said as if Scarlett wasn't sitting right there. "Kevin supposed to be watching him but only God knows how that's going down." She grabbed her towel and walked away, her wet feet slapping against the floor.

"I'm going to help her," Scarlett said as she followed.

Bambi and I sat across from each other. She took a deep breath and said, "Kevin has fucked around on me too. Even had a baby situation outside of our marriage. You know all of this. His infidelity hurt but I made a decision to forgive him. It doesn't mean I forgot, Race, I'm stronger than that. I just forgave him." She touched my arm. "At the end of the day I told myself I was going to deal with it or not. Since I knew I was not going to live without him I did what I had to do. That meant not bringing up what he did every five minutes though."

"I will never forgive Ramirez."

"People make mistakes, Race. The same thing could happen to you."

"Never. I would never sleep around while dedicated to him."

She sighed and rose out the water, wrapping her pink towel around her body. "Just remember when you're pointing your index finger at someone else your other fingers will always be pointed back at you." She paused. "Now I gotta get some rest to clear my mind. As you can imagine it's been a long night." She turned and walked away.

Ramirez and me were facing one another on the bed within our dark bedroom. Tension in the house was high as everyone wondered what would happen as a result of Abd kidnapping Bambi and then fucking with our mental by releasing her and letting her come back home.

It was all a game to Abd.

And he was scaring the shit out of me.

To make matters worse Scarlett was walking around with Master who was not willing to quiet down since he arrived. I think she was horrified to be a mother. That smile at the door when she first brought him home was the only thing he gave us because the rest of the time he was pure hell. Crying at the top of his lungs for what seemed like hours.

Still, the little boy was beyond adorable and looked so much like Scarlett and Camp that it was insane. But the kid seemed on edge. Maybe he sensed we were dangerous and wanted to be with his reverend family. As far away from our hot asses as possible.

I can't say that I blame him.

"I want you to know that I will always protect you, Race." Ramirez wiped my hair from my face. "You know that right? I'll kill Abd before I let him touch you."

Fuck is this nigga talking about?

My eyes remained closed. "I'm not weak anymore." I pulled the sheet up to my chin and yawned in his face. "There's no need to protect me. Try to protect yourself."

"Whether you need me or not you're my wife. And I need you to know that I love you."

I opened my eyes, rolled them and sighed. "Drop it. You're the talking-ess man I've ever come past in my life. Why you got so much word play for me these days?" I closed my lids again. "Please, go back to sleep."

Suddenly I felt his hand on my breasts and when I opened my eyes again he was running his thumb over my nipple. It could've been a rat walking over me and would've felt the same way.

Disgusting.

I shoved his hand away. "Get off me! I'm not in the mood tonight."

"Then when you gonna be in the fucking mood?"

"Never. Now go back to sleep."

He jumped up, grabbed his robe and walked toward the door. "If you don't want to be my wife I wish you'd just tell me. Instead of acting like there's hope between us, Race, because I can't take it anymore."

"Everything's not about you."

"Then what's it about if it's not about a Kennedy? I made you my wife to play your position and you not doing it." He pointed at her. "This not gonna go down forever."

"You so fucking arrogant." I laughed. "Just leave it alone, Ramirez. Your mood swings not getting to me anymore."

"You know what, I'm done fighting with you tonight." He turned around to leave.

"Where you going?" I frowned.

"To hold my little nephew. Maybe I can put a smile on his face since I can't put one on yours."

RAMIREZ

Ramirez walked into Scarlett's room just as Master was kicking and screaming, making it obvious that he didn't fuck with his real mother in any shape, form or fashion.

"Can I help?" Ramirez asked entering the room.

Scarlett turned around, saw Ramirez and cried. He rushed up to her, eased Master out of her arms and held her with the other. "It's gonna be okay. Just give it some time. Don't nothing happen overnight."

"I can't do this, Ramirez. I'm not nobody's mother. I mean look at me." She separated from him and wiped the tears streaming down her face. "I'm awful at this and I'm awful at life."

He frowned. "Stop talking like that. You can do this."

"No I can't! Look at him, he doesn't even like me."

Ramirez grabbed her hand, walked her over to the sofa and they both sat down. He squeezed her fingers softly and said, "Listen to my voice and hear nothing else. Okay?"

She looked into his eyes, hers beet red due to her pressure rising. "O...okay, Ramirez. Whatever you say."

"I want you to take five deep breaths." He whispered. "And make them slow, nobody's rushing you."

"It won't work."

He frowned. "Yes it will. Babies know when you're a ball of negative energy and they want you to take charge." Ramirez looked down at Master who had already settled his spirit since being in his arm. "You have to convince babies, non verbally that you can take care of them. That you

By **T. Styles** 73

can protect them." He wiped a band of her red hair behind her ear. "Now breathe but do it slowly."

Unhurriedly she took the breaths not really believing they would work until the third breath calmed her soul. When she reached the fifth he looked into her eyes and said, "You ready to hold him again?"

Scarlett looked at Master and nodded. "But he looks so peaceful, maybe I should leave him alone."

He smiled and sat the little boy on her lap anyway. She tried desperately to maintain her composure but felt herself unraveling until he placed his hand on her warm cream-colored thigh. "Relax, Scarlett. He's your son. Them mothafuckas who had him before can't come in between that, I don't care how long he lived with them. You gave birth to this baby. He is from you and my brother. That makes him a king, born to a queen."

She nodded and took one more breath. This time when she looked at Master he was smiling. A single tear fell down her cheek and he wiped it away with his thumb. "You see...he knows who his mother really is."

Feeling more confident, she walked Master to his crib because his eyes were closing. Slowly she placed him down and stole a few moments to look at his peaceful face.

When he was sleep Ramirez walked behind her and stared at the curves of her body. Now it was time for other matters. Grown folk business. She could feel the heat off his body and the sexual tension he was throwing her way.

He wanted to fuck.

She did too. Although she tried her best to fight the feeling.

"Why are you doing this to me?" She asked.

"Doing what?"

"Why are you making yourself my hero?" She turned around and looked up at him. "It's like you want me to fall...to fall..."

"In love?"

"Yes!" She said louder than she intended. "I mean...you can't be this person for me. I don't want to be in a situation where I depend on you emotionally. You don't belong to me, Ramirez and you never will. Don't force me to believe that you do."

"You're my family, Scarlett. I'm supposed to love you and you're supposed to love me back. What's wrong with that?"

"You know what I mean." She walked away and he grabbed her hand, kissed her lips and looked down at her. "I dream about you. I think about that moment we shared together. But if I'm causing you this much pain I won't touch you again unless you ask, Scarlett because that's how much I care."

Her body trembled and so did Race's as she hid out in the hall and watched the alarming scene from the doorway.

CHAPTER SIX

ABD

A bd was sitting on the sofa with his son Jawad in his living room, discussing their lucrative oil business back in Saudi Arabia. Within seconds Abd abruptly switched the convo to his son's future wife.

"So, son, Rana tells me she's been unhappy the past few days. Says she doesn't know how to please you. That nothing she does seems to work. She's considering going back home." Abd sat back and crossed his legs. "What's troubling you, that you believe our success and that wife of yours isn't part of the plan?"

Jawad looked away, leaned back in his seat and sighed. "I'm sorry, father, it's just that—"

"I need you to make nice with your future wife, son." Abd said harshly. "Your marriage will make this family the richest in the world. Isn't that what you want?" He gave him strong eye contact.

"I will, father, I don't mean to sound ungrateful. I'm happy about the choice you made but—"

"But what?"

"She smells funny."

Abd eyes widened. "What does that mean?"

"She doesn't wash properly and she stinks up the sheets." He shook his head. "I don't know if it's her private area or her armpits but she's nasty and I hate having her around me. It drives me insane, father."

He boomed with laughter. "So send her to the other room. You shouldn't have to be subjected to her odors while you sleep or are resting."

Jawad's eyes widened. "I can do that?"

"Son, do what you must to make this marriage occur successfully. Do what you have to, to mold her into what you want. Jawad nodded and Abd said, "So you've tasted the goods already and they were sour, huh?" Abd chuckled.

"Father, I'm serious."

Abd removed the smile from his face. "I know you're serious and so am I. Remember who I am. And remember when I ask you a question I demand an answer. No matter how frivolous you may think it is."

Jawad sent his gaze to the floor. "No, I haven't tested them just yet. Like I said, her body odor is too horrendous."

Abd smiled again. "Well make her wash and then try her out. Give her a spin and see if she's too your liking."

"And if she isn't?"

"Then make her into what you want. Teach her how to be. A woman is like a mound of clay." He made a fist. "They can be shaped into whatever you desire because unlike men who require money for survival, women have been created needing the weakest of all life's necessities. Love. Convince her you care and she'll be whatever you desire. This my son, I promise."

"I understand, father."

"Then go."

Jawad stood up and shook his father's hand before walking away.

Jawad moped into the bedroom where his future wife stood waiting, knitting an aqua colored sweater for the baby she was sure would come soon.

It wasn't like she didn't try to make Jawad not desire her. She purposely got into the shower being careful to clean *everything but her vagina and ass. The plan was to convince Jawad to send her back to her family in Saudi Arabia after being frustrated with her but she didn't take into account Abd's powerful presence. He would rather kill her than to lose the access to money her family would bring.*

Using yarn of a mixture of pale aqua and yellow she placed her artwork down when he entered. Quickly she stood on her feet as he sat on the edge of the bed. He could smell her pussy the moment he walked into the room.

"Anything I can do?" Her hands clasped in front of her. "Maybe I can make you Shawarma? I've already started to prepare the meal."

Slowly he looked up at her, grabbed her by her long black hair and brought her to her knees. "Jawad, don't hurt me again. Please."

He squeezed her chin, pulled it down and stuck his fingers into her mouth. "Your beauty disgusts me. Look at you. You get to move along in life, having whatever you want just because of how you look? When I have to take my father's games, educate myself in the business and fight for survival? Just because I'm a man? Women are nothing but disgusting creatures taking up space." He removed his fingers and wiped her own spit on her cheek. "You aren't any different."

Not knowing what to say she said, "I'm so sorry, Jawad. I wish I didn't sicken you because I want nothing more than to love you. To be what you envision."

"Remove my shoes." He released her hair and she quickly untied the sneakers he used to run earlier that morning. He wasn't wearing any socks so his toes were free and he wiggled them around to stretch out the cracks.

With his shoes on the floor she said, "Anything else?"

"Suck my toes."

She looked down at his feet, the soft sting of vinegar-dried sweat already occupying her nostrils. "But...should I clean them – "

SLAP!

She held her face and massaged the stinging sensation jolting through her cheek after he smacked her. "I said suck my toes and don't question me again. EVER! You will learn what I prefer and you will not like it."

Rana lowered her head and starting with the right toe on his left foot, sucked the musty sweat off one by one. As he looked down at her he smiled thinking that the best part of this new marriage will be exhibiting the hate he had for his father onto her.

After all Jawad was a gay man.

And he despised the world because of it.

CHAPTER SEVEN

RACE

I was pacing my bedroom floor, gun in hand trying to think about who I would kill first.

Please God; give me the strength not to commit a double homicide tonight.

I can't believe this is happening. My chest tightened. This nigga had the nerve to beg me for some pussy and then when I refused, go upstairs to fuck my friend? My temples throbbed and I tried to stroke them with my free hand but the pain would not disappear. The betrayal was so heavy I felt weighted down and I could no longer move.

Flopping on the bed, I looked out into the room and it felt like it was spinning. Why didn't I see this coming? She was a beautiful newly single woman right in this house. How long had this been happening? The only reason I left instead of doing what my spirit wanted was because I needed a weapon but now I was feeling something else.

The sting of betrayal.

My mother always said, never allow a single woman to stay in your house longer than a weekend. And yet Scarlett was here for life.

When I received a text I picked up the phone and looked down at it. It was from my New Friend and I realized I welcomed the distraction. It wouldn't take my mind off of what I'd seen but it may calm me for the moment.

At least I hoped.

Quickly I walked into the bathroom, slammed the door and flopped on the toilet seat.

Text Message

New Friend: I miss talkin' 2 U.

Me: We need to speak. On the phone.

New Friend: Sure. U okay?

Me: Too much to say over text.

He didn't respond right away and I felt my heart dropping deeper into the pit of my stomach. We agreed that we would wait until the right time to speak on the phone and I hoped that my desperation in the moment didn't scare him away. Or worse, turn him off.

All I needed was a friend.

Someone objective because in that moment I made a decision.

Ramirez and Scarlett would die before the end of the night.

I would've spoken to Bambi but the loyalty I had for the Kennedy family had me not wanting to get her involved, forcing her to choose sides. Besides, I didn't need her trying to talk me out of my plan so it would be a waste. Although now that I think about it, when we were in the truck Bambi was trying to tell me something but I couldn't receive her.

Could it be that she knew about Scarlett and Ramirez all along?

Now I was angry with her too.

I need to breathe.

God, please help me.

Text Message

New Friend: Can you call me now?

Me: Yes.

I looked at the phone took a deep breath and dialed the number. The moment he answered I felt relief. His voice was heavy with base, confidence and sexiness. The thing is all he said was, 'Hello'.

"So before you say anything," he said next. "Are you gonna ask if I'm one of the actors or the director?"

I smiled and considering what I'd just seen with the betrayal that's saying a lot about his personality. He knew how to make me giddy despite the hate swimming in my body in the moment. "No. I don't care. I just need someone to talk to right now."

He laughed. "I like, I like. You're keeping the mystery of us alive."

"Yes. I guess you can say that." I paused and wiped my hair back. "Plus I don't want whatever we got going on destroyed by a bunch of questions. Anyway I'm calling for something else."

He exhaled and I wondered how warm his breath would feel against my cheek. "So talk to me. What has you up in arms, Race Kennedy?"

I looked around, stood up and reviewed my reflection in the mirror. Now that I had him on the phone I wasn't sure if I wanted to tell him that my husband didn't love me anymore. And that I may have been the cause because my pride would not allow me to let him fuck me. Or that he was sleeping with my sister-in-law.

This entire ordeal was muddy as fuck.

By **T. Styles** 85

"I have a dilemma. And I don't know how to handle it." I told him. "I was hoping you could help."

"Well...does this dilemma involve someone you love?"

My eyes narrowed. "Yes."

He laughed but not loudly or out of disrespect I'm sure. "If it involves someone you love that changes things. You know that right?"

I sat on the edge of the cool tub and looked down at my red polished toes. "I know. That's why it burns so badly."

"Does your dilemma involve another person? That you also love?"

"If I wasn't sure I'd think you knew what was happening to me already." I bit my lip after a flash of them together entered my mind again.

He chuckled. "No...I don't know what you're about to drop on me. Not yet anyway. I'm just giving you the chance to keep as much privacy as you want by not giving too much detail. I don't want you regretting what you say to me in the morning."

Damn, I'm feeling this man already.

"Thank you."

"No problem. Now talk to me."

I stood up, flipped on the switch to heat the floors and paced. "Someone I love betrayed me with someone else I love." I paused. "And everything in me wants to kill them both. Tonight. In fact I made up my mind already. I guess I wanted to talk to someone about it first." I can't believe I was so honest but at the same time relief moved through me.

"I've been that mad but let me say this before you make a move. If you kill them, especially with you being angry, you'll feel guilty soon thereafter. I know you may not think you will but trust me guilt will come back for you. It always does. But if you make them pay in another way, the satisfaction can last for a lifetime."

I thought about what he said and the way he said it. His tone was creepy but his words rang true and called out to my soul. "What are you suggesting I do? Because I'm not letting it go."

"If these are people you love then that must mean you know them well. Instead of killing them take your time to get revenge. They say revenge is a dish best served cold because you don't eat the meal when it's hot and you're angry. You wait until you've had time to sit with it for a while to think of the best plan. When you think it's time, write a list of what they love the most and when you have it in your possession take everything from them. Leave nothing on the table."

I stopped pacing. "Wow, remind me to never get on your bad side."

He laughed. "Impossible for you to be on that side." He paused. "Plus I just want you to have what you really desire without getting time for murder. You think that it's blood you want but when you consider your predicament, whatever it may be, you'll find out it's the furthest thing from the truth. You want them to feel pain? Emotional pain for betraying you. And what better way to give them that, except that they be alive long enough for your plans to go through? Take your time, Race. Don't move fast."

Strangely, just thinking about taking my time was getting me excited already. "You're right." I nodded.

"I'm here if you need me, Race."

Although I received the comfort I wanted from him I desired to hang around a little longer on the call just to hear his voice. "Do you have anyone? In your life you care about? Or are serious with?"

"I thought we wouldn't go there until we were ready."

"I'm ready now."

"You're in pain and you're looking for a ride out." He paused. "I can't be that for you, not in this way. When we meet and discuss our lives I want the time to be right."

I shook my head. "All you did just now was make me want to know you even more."

"Then my job is done." He paused. "Good night, beautiful. Soon we'll talk. In the meantime think about the ones who wronged you and what it will take to get the revenge you need. I'm here if you want ideas."

Now he was scaring me and yet I couldn't turn away. "Thank you."

"Thank me by striking back. The calculating way."

When he ended the call I slid out of the bedroom. Part of my anger returned when I saw that Ramirez hadn't come back to our room, or our bed.

Fuck this nigga!

I had to stay unemotional even though I thought I was about to say fuck it and approach him anyway. Instead I took five deep breaths like Ramirez had taught me in the past and relaxed.

It was like turning the eye off under a pot of boiling water.

I sat on the edge of the bed and looked ahead at the wall. What do you want Ramirez? And what do you want Scarlett?

Whatever it is. I'm taking it all away.

An hour later he returned to our room. Soiled with her perfume, her body fluids and of course lies.

He showered first.

The telltale sign of a man who's been cheating and although I wanted to scream at the top of my lungs I maintained my composure. Even when he raised the sheets, lowered them over his whorish body and snuggled close to me. With his arm resting heavily on my waist he kissed me on the back. "I love you, Race."

God, please help me!

I bit my bottom lip. So hard this time I drew blood, the salty fluid coating my tongue and flowing down the back of my throat. "I'm sorry for hurting you, Ramirez. I know you need me now more than ever, with Camp being gone. I've been so selfish I don't see how you can stand me."

"You've been there don't say—"

"I am going to say it because it's a wife's duty to express how much she cares about her man and I haven't done that for you lately. But I want you to know that I'm awake now and you'll see a change in me. A firm one."

"Wow, that's what I always wanted to hear."

To add to the ruse I turned around and looked into his eyes. The green glare from the LED alarm clock allowed me to see his sneaky face. He was a monster, the handsome, sneaky, big dick kind. "You're everything to me, Ramirez." I paused. "You believe me don't you? You believe that as long as your are faithful and true I'll be faithful and truer to you?"

Guilt appeared to weigh down his words because he didn't answer right away. And since I knew the truth about him fucking Scarlett I waited quietly. Refusing to say anything, which would allow him off the hook.

"I believe you, Race. And I'm sorry for allowing her into our marriage."

"Her?" I said in a naive tone. The question was like a double entendre. I knew who he was speaking about but it could apply to Scarlett or Carey considering what I knew.

"Scar...I mean Carey."

I smiled.

He was so drunk with another woman's love he was about to say her name in our marital bed. Getting him back would be more than an eye for an eye type of situation. It would be pleasurable. "I love you so much, Ramirez." I closed my eyes and kissed his dirty lips. "I'm gonna have a lot of fun showing you."

CHAPTER EIGHT

BAMBI

I woke up with a bad feeling in the pit of my gut. Something terrible was going to happen today. The moment I rolled out of bed and walked to the bathroom Kevin got up too and followed me.

What was on his mind?

I sat on the toilet and pee trickled out of my body and splashed inside the bowl and yet he continued to stare like my face changed. "Kevin, what is this about? I know you haven't been asleep because whenever I turned over in the middle of the night you were looking at me."

His jaw twitched and he leaned against the wall. "When you gonna tell me what really happened with Abd? Huh? Because what you saying don't make sense. I thought about it all night and can't think of one scenario where he would let you go."

My eyes widened and I let out a loud laugh. I couldn't believe he was coming at me like this. "Wait, are you serious? I got snatched out my truck and you blaming me?" I pointed at myself.

"Bambi, stop fucking with me. What really happened when he kidnapped you? I didn't want to say this in front of the family but I know they're wondering too. Because it doesn't make a lot of sense that he would let you go when he had you where he wanted you. He could've kept you, extorted money out of us and everything."

I hit the toilet paper roll a few times and snatched off a piece. "Kevin, I could've been killed. The last thing I want to do is argue with you about what might have happened." I wiped my pussy, dropped the tissue and flushed the toilet before moving to the sink to wash my hands.

"I know them middle eastern niggas." He stood behind me. "And they rape bitches like you. Did he touch you? In any way?"

"First off a middle eastern nigga sounds strange so I want you to never say that shit again. Secondly what do you think happened? Because it's obvious that you have an opinion."

"I think you did what you had to and if that's the case I wish you'd just tell me instead of letting me find out from another source. We always keep shit one hundred with each other."

"Do we?" I said thinking about the bitch he fucked some years back.

"Bambi..."

I dried my hands, walked out of the bedroom and flopped on the edge of the bed. "Kevin, I'm not well enough emotionally to fight you. Nor do I want to. I told you everything he said and now I'm here and alive. I'm happy about that. Aren't you? I mean can't that be enough?" Suddenly my cell phone kicked off and I reached over to grab it. When I turned the phone up I saw Sarge's number. "What up, Sarge?"

"First off how are you, Bambi? I've been worried sick but nobody would let me talk to you."

"I'm sorry, Sarge. I took a few pills to sleep and was out of it last night. Plus the family wanted me to get some rest so no one wanted to wake me." I paused. "But why do you sound frantic?"

"I hate to do this to you but I have more bad news."

I stood up. "What is it now?"

"Our men are dead...it's a massacre out here in these streets!" He yelled. "I've never seen anything like this."

I rubbed the back of my neck. "What you talking about?"

"Everybody's gone, Bambi. Before I called you I checked on all of our blocks and every nigga grinding is gone in D.C. The way it happened reminds me of when we were in Saudi Arabia. They were on some sniper shit, taking out one after another of our men."

Kevin snatched the phone out of my hand and placed the call on speaker. "What about our Baltimore soldiers? They hit too?"

"No, I believe they got word and took cover," Sarge continued. "But everybody else is gone, bosses."

Kevin looked at me and shook his head. "Go to the Emergency Room and we'll be there in an hour," he told him.

"Okay..." Sarge ended the call and Kevin tossed my phone on the bed.

When the line went dead he looked at me. "I guess you got your answer, Kevin," I said with an attitude. "He didn't kill or fuck me because he had another plan. To shut down our operation from the outside. He's playing games. He wants the take down to be slow and painful."

Me, Kevin, Race, Ramirez, Scarlett, Bradley and Denim walked into the Emergency Room. One of our female soldiers watched over Master at the compound.

The location was in a small underground warehouse we used to stash weapons sometimes. We were all strapped and ready for a street war if need be an there were five men covering the front and five covering the back to make sure nobody got in our hideaway aka THE EMERGENCY ROOM.

Inside were Sarge and three of our trusted men and they didn't look as confident as they did in the past, especially Sarge. When I looked at him I was shocked because although he was much older, probably in his fifties, his face took on a deeper age in the moment. And I believe I saw a few gray hairs sprouting around the front of his hairline that weren't there before.

We sat around the oval table and Sarge sighed deeply before talking. "Prior to this shit tonight I spent my career in the army."

"You don't have to tell me, Sarge," I reminded him. "I was with you for at least a few of them years."

"I know, Bambi. And my statement was built with no disrespect, boss, but I wanted to give you an idea of what we dealing with out there. I'm talking about an organized attack on our men. They had a firing squad for every man on our D.C. blocks and they activated that hit at the same time causing mass destruction." He paused and wiped the sweat from his brow. "Our boys aren't equipped for this type of war. They thug niggas. We haven't trained 'em for it. I mean, they're good for gun on gun attacks but this shit was strategic. Armies are in training for years to gain the skills necessary to fight Abd."

I looked down. "I hired someone to find out more Intel on Abd and his D.C. presence."

"I know, Roman called already to get some information. I think she's perfect because she works quietly and alone."

"But it's going to be a slow process, Sarge. Roman is good but until we find out where Abd is we have to lay low."

Sarge looked down. "I have always supported the Kennedy King movement." He focused back on us. "You all know that..."

"So why you saying that, nigga?" Kevin said. "We said we have you so you gonna have to ride on our word."

"It's not that...it's just that I'm scared for my family," he said focusing on his knuckles. "Working with you has allowed me to live in luxury but not security. I don't have an underground compound like the Kennedy's to retreat to when times are rough like this."

"Why it sound like you hating?" Ramirez asked.

"I'm thinking the same thing." Race said. "If you feel you need more security then say it, Sarge. We prefer our executives to be real with us and not beat around the bush. Besides, it takes too much time."

Sarge looked around. "I'm born for combat. Even if I wanted to hide the fight in my blood won't allow such a cowardly act. But my wife and daughter, well, I need them safe. I can't move like you want on the streets while I'm worrying about them."

I looked around at *my family*. I knew how he felt. And since this was mostly my fault since I killed Mitch I felt obliged to help him. "So you want them to stay with us? At our home?"

"I wouldn't ask you this, Bambi, if I wasn't genuinely concerned. But, yes. I just want my daughter and her mother to stay with you. At least until this blows over. Knowing they're there means I'll work overtime."

I looked around the room because I couldn't do this by myself. If we were going to take insiders into our home, into the sanctity of our privacy, I needed the okay from everyone.

"I'm fine with it," Race said.

"I'm good too." Ramirez responded.

I'm not sure but I could've sworn I heard Race say, *'I bet you are'*, after Ramirez spoke. But maybe I'm tripping.

Bradley looked at Denim and she said, "We fucks with Sarge. So you know we good."

I focused my attention on Scarlett. "I'm just happy to still be a part of this family. After Camp died I thought me and my baby would have to go at it alone so whatever you guys need from me I'm here."

I thought I heard Race say something under her breath again but when I looked at her she had her game face on and was staring at Sarge. Something was definitely going on in the air but for now it was about business.

I looked over at Kevin. "What do you think?"

Kevin focused on Sarge. "We can provide them protection but if for whatever reason it doesn't work they'll have to find some place else to stash because the last thing we need is problems in our home right now. We have enough of that as you can imagine."

"I'll talk to them," Sarge said happily. "Trust me, there won't be an issue on my end." He stabbed a stiff finger into the table.

"Then they'll be safe. In the Kennedy way."

"Thank you," Sarge said excitedly. "Thank you so much."

"With this privilege much is expected." I reminded him. "The fact that we're offering your family solitude means you have to keep your eyes on the blocks. Use your skills to find out all you can about Abd, Sarge. We counting on you."

"Bambi, I'm already on it. Before coming here I made sure that our Bmore soldiers stayed clear of the streets until we can sort this mess out. The only problem I'm having is from Yvette and Carissa."

I frowned. "What's their issue?"

"Apparently they had a little upset in the property they run in D.C. over the winter. To offset the issues they gave a lower price on their product, basically under cutting themselves."

"You mean Marjorie Gardens?" Race asked.

Sarge nodded. "Yes, so they been trying to order large shipments to get things rolling again and that last package moved quicker than expected. Now they dry."

"Where is Mercedes?" Bambi asked.

"I think she's out the game."

I laughed.

"But they didn't order from us over the winter," Race interjected.

I scratched my head. "Exactly."

Sarge shrugged. "I'm not sure what went down. All I know is that they tried to place a call for another order and Scarlett told them they'd have to wait."

"I had to," Scarlett advised. "Because things are moving crazy right now and Bambi told me to hold off after she was kidnapped."

"I get that but I think they believe it's personal," Sarge said.

"Tell Yvette to get in contact with me," I said. "If she has any questions I'll be happy to address them personally." I fucked with Yvette and her crew but I can't lie, part of me thinks that Yvette's jealous of me and my reign. Shit ain't the way it used to be in the Emerald City days. Around D.C., I'm king.

"I'll tell her," Sarge nodded.

"And I'll let her know stuff ain't personal if she calls back too," Scarlett said.

"Until then we need to all be very careful. We were able to win the war with the Russians and in turn got involved in something much darker," I continued.

"Keep your heads low and be ready. And, Sarge, let our soldiers know too. This is a state of emergency. We are officially under attack."

CHAPTER NINE

RACE

Standing in front of the mirror I took a look at myself. Red lipstick was smeared over my pouty mouth. My hair was dressed in a loose curl bob that covered the sides of my cheek, brushing my shoulders. Black eye shadow kissed my eyelids making me look sinister.

I loved what I was seeing.

Darkness as I revealed hints of my evil intentions.

Today was the day I would activate my four-step plan of revenge and I thought about it all night and all morning. It didn't take me long to figure out what each of them wanted and even shorter to come up with a plan. You see, they're predictable like that, wearing their wants and their needs on their sleeves for the world to see.

I'm positive that when I was done with both Scarlett and Ramirez, their lives would be ruined forever.

Taking one last look at my physique, I rubbed my hands down my blue jeans and walked into Scarlett's room where she was sitting on the sofa. This whore had fucked my husband and now she had the nerve to be sitting, doing regular shit.

Funky bitch.

She focused on me and I quickly wiped the look of disgust off my face so she couldn't sense my motives. It was probably comforting to her because when she first gazed my way she looked as if she'd seen a ghost.

No, my dear, Scarlett. I won't confront you about your betrayal just yet.

"Wow, you look, sexy," she said. "Going somewhere?"

"Of course not," I walked further inside. "After Bambi's kidnapping we're on official lockdown. You were in that meeting. We will never see the light of day," I giggled. "But a girl can still play dress up can't she?" I raised my arms and spun around.

She smiled. "Of course."

"Listen, I'm here because Bambi wanted me to remind you to tell all of the soldiers that sales would be suspended until further notice. We can't fulfill any orders until this thing with Abd blows over."

Scarlett sighed. "Yes, of course. I've been letting everyone know but people aren't as sympathetic with what we got going on as I hoped. Do you think this will work?" She asked.

What do I give a fuck? I really want to talk about you sleeping with my husband. I thought.

"What you mean, Scarlett? By if it will work?"

She shrugged. "What's to stop them from finding product from an outside source? The demand doesn't go away when we do. I learned that from you guys. Seems so risky to me. And I know I'm not a part of the business back office matters but still. I think we're shooting ourselves in the foot."

"Can you handle this or not?" I frowned.

"Of course!"

"Then we better not lose business." I pointed at her. "That could be a problem for you."

"You're right. I'll make it work by thinking of a good enough explanation." When Master cooed in his crib she got up, pat his back and he went to sleep.

"Wow, I notice you're getting better with him. A few days ago you had your hands full but now…"

She exhaled. "I don't know about good. I'm just trying to remain calm whenever I'm near him because he seems to feed off me in some ways. That's crazy the way babies are."

"And how does one do that?" I asked. "I'm talking about staying calm?"

"I just take deep breaths and do my best to relax."

Wow. Ramirez even taught her his breathing techniques.

I nodded. "Now that I think about it I think I remember Ramirez telling Bambi the same thing when the twins were young, about the deep breaths and all. He said it's always important to be calm and strong when you hold a baby. Because you can fuck up their energy if you don't. Apparently his sitter use to do the same thing to them when they were kids and he never forgot it."

Her eyes widened and she seemed cramped. Maybe because she unknowingly let on that Ramirez had taught her something he shared with others. Which brought more attention to the connection they weren't supposed to be having.

Dirty bitch.

"Oh, maybe he did tell me that too and I don't remember." She scratched her scalp. "Things have been moving so fast since Master came home." She looked around as if she was searching for a pot to throw up in. "Excuse me for a minute, Race but I'll be back." She hurried off.

When she was gone I walked over to the crib and apologized in advance for pulling Master in on my future plans. But revenge involved many players and I needed all hands on deck, including his tiny ones.

But first, let me activate step one.

I looked back toward the bathroom and when I saw Scarlett wasn't coming I picked up the Dope Phone, put in a number and attempted to redirect all calls to the burner cell phone number I just purchased which sat in my room. I messed up the first few times and finally got it right just as Scarlett was walking back in.

"Did I miss a call?" she asked when she saw me holding the phone.

I placed the handset down. "No, I thought you did but I was hearing things." I walked up to her. "Scarlett, I know we haven't been as close as I would like but I want you to know that I always looked at you as a sister. The fact that you're white and I'm black means nothing. We are closer than blood could ever bind us and I want you to remember that."

I saw her swallow, her pale throat bubbling up before smoothing out again. "I...I think of you as a sister too."

"Good." I kissed her on the cheek leaving my red lips on her whorish face. "Well let me go downstairs and prepare dinner. It's my night to cook and Ramirez gets so angry when I don't get that time in the kitchen. He really loves my meals you know?"

She nodded. "I'm sure he does."

"Well, I'll see you in an hour. I'm making tacos and margaritas tonight. You're gonna love them."

"I always do, Race. Thank you."

I smiled and walked away, secretly thinking of the day when she would die a cold death.

SCARLETT

I paced the floor, my nerves so bad I felt myself trembling. Ramirez walked into my room and closed the door behind him. His strides were smooth as if he didn't have a care in the world. The moment he stepped up to me I said, "She knows about us. I'm positive."

He laughed once. "What you talking about? Race and I haven't been as good as we are now in years. She apologized for acting like a bitch over the past few weeks and everything. Trust me, I have her under my Kennedy thumb."

"She's too nice, Ramirez." I warned. "And I don't know how she could find out but trust me when I say she knows. I mean look at my face." I pointed at the lipstick stain she left. "She kissed my cheek and shit. Since when does she kiss me? This ain't adding up."

"First off it's not a crime to kiss you. You're my friend and I kiss you all the time."

"Ramirez!"

"Stop getting worked up. Besides, my wife would never think we would be capable of anything like this. Not me and you anyway. Instead of fighting we should be supporting each other and enjoying our time together. We're in lockdown, Scarlett. Let's have fun with it." He rubbed my shoulders and I looked into his eyes. I felt in that moment that his seduction went deeper than our sexual attraction for one another.

Somewhere low inside of him, he wanted to get back at Race and he was using me to do it. Even if he didn't know his own motives.

"Just go, Ramirez." I took a deep breath. "I — "

Suddenly I felt his warm finger stroking my naked pussy, pressing against my clit making it tingle, causing me to juice up instantly. He had snuck his fingers up my dress and I hadn't even seen him move that quickly.

How did he do that? How was he so brave? He was so spontaneous and fun that he messed me up. There was excitement in his sexual mood swings and I didn't have that with Camp. Before I could beg him to stop he had picked me up, pushed me against the wall and entered my pussy.

My legs wrapped around his waist and his strokes were slow at first before moving quickly. Each thrust of his dick inside my body meant a brush against my throbbing hot clit. He knew how to fuck me and I felt my body heat up and my legs quiver as he took control.

So forceful.

So sexual.

He was dangerous.

"Damn, Scarlett, you wet already," he whispered breathing onto my neck.

I bit my bottom lip and pressed my fingers into his back; careful not to scratch him and leave additional traces of our affair although it felt so good I wanted to draw blood. "Give me that black dick, Ramirez. Please."

"So you want this black dick, huh?" he said in my ear. "You want this dick in this white pussy?"

"Fuck this pussy," I said sucking on his earlobe. "Cum all in this pink pussy, Ramirez. Please…"

"Fuck, don't stop talking, Scarlett," he begged, his breaths heavy with passion. "And keep that pussy open too, just like that, baby."

Somehow we made our way to the bed and it lasted all of five minutes but it felt like an eternity.

"Mmmmmmm, fuck," he said as he came inside of me. "Damn, you felt so good."

Slowly he raised his head and looked into my eyes. Wiping my red hair behind my ear he said, "You see…we can't stop doing this. We move too good together, don't you understand that?"

I did recognize the chemistry we had but guilt was fucking with me. I wish I could care as little as he apparently did about our nastiness.

I smiled and walked to the bathroom. He followed me. Grabbing my washcloth I turned on the sink faucet and allowed the hot water to run over it, burning my fingertips in the process, turning them cherry red.

He stood behind me.

Smiling & watching.

"You enjoying this more than you should," I said.

"Is that a problem? That I like us together?"

"And what does that mean, you like us together?" I paused, looking at his reflection in the mirror. "This may be fun for you but I can't see doing this forever, Ramirez. It's not like you're going to leave Race and I wouldn't want you to."

"I will never leave her." He said, his face contorting into something evil, something violent. "As a matter of fact don't even bring it up in discussion again because it will never happen." He pointed at me.

I turned around, took a deep breath and gazed up at him. "I said I would *never* want you to do that, Ramirez. I just need you to realize it's wrong of you to force me to have feelings for you by coming into my room whenever you want. Just because you're a Kennedy. I have no privacy with you."

He rubbed my shoulders. "Just go with the flow. You need this dick as much as I need that pussy right now. We'll figure out everything else as we go along. Okay?" He kissed me on the cheek and I slapped him because he wouldn't take me seriously.

He frowned and I slapped him again.

And again.

And again.

He took each blow and grinned. When I was done he said, "I know you and Camp use to fight and fuck but if you ever put your hands on me again I will kill you." He stormed out.

CHAPTER TEN
RAMIREZ

*W*hen Ramirez walked down the staircase toward the kitchen he smiled at the smell of a hot meal tantalizing his senses. It had been a while since Race cooked and it always made him angry when she refused to take her place in the kitchen during her meal preparation week.

Luckily for him tonight was different.

When he first married her she was all, cooking, all fucking and all serving. But ever since she started moving a brick of coke or two with the family she would bribe someone else to cook when it was her time.

All he wanted was some semblance of the wife he used to have and he had a feeling based on the conversation they had the other night in the bed that he would finally get his way. Sure he had some pussy upstairs and some pussy downstairs but didn't his lineage afford him as many women as he desired?

After all, as he told everybody who would listen, he was a Kennedy.

When he bent the corner that led to the kitchen he heard soft laughter. Stepping closer he saw Race and Bradley laughing it up by the stove. She was stirring taco sauce in a pan and Bradley was standing next to her, looking down in her face, chuckling like she was a one bitch comedy show. His body was too close for Ramirez's liking and because he was cheating himself he didn't trust anybody or any situation.

Something didn't feel right.

For a second he took in the scene but remained where he was. His feet felt like cinder blocks holding him down as his breath quickened. Sure it was fucked up for him to be jealous since he had in house pussy from his brother's wife, but this was different. He was not about to let Race fuck with another Kennedy in their home.

Not on his watch.

Not on his wife.

"Why you get me fucked up off that sherry?" Bradley asked Race. "I'm gonna have to watch you." He pointed at her. "You dangerous."

Race smiled as she turned up the flirting game, brushing against him as they stood over the stove. She knew Ramirez was watching. She always knew when he was watching her. Her perrifpheal vision was legendary.

If two different people judged the scene they would have different opinions. One might say they were friends laughing it up in the kitchen. But the other one would say they were minutes away from having a sex fest on the kitchen floor and that's how Ramirez felt.

"All I said was taste a little bit of sherry." She giggled. "You the one who turned the bottle upside down and poured it in your throat." She laughed harder. "I told you, you could get fucked up off of it but you didn't believe me."

"Yeah, well I should've listened to you." He boomed with laughter. "But I can't lie, your taco sauce tastes good."

Her eyebrows rose. "You mean you didn't ruin my recipe by sucking down most of the sherry? I almost didn't have enough messing with you."

Bradley dipped his finger into the sauce and licked it. "I'm telling you it's right, Race. Just needs a little salt that's all."

Race stopped stirring, turned around and hit his arm playfully. "So now you gonna tell me how to cook too?"

"Ow, that hurt," he rubbed his bicep. "I didn't know you had a left hook on you."

"There's a lot of stuff you don't know about her," Ramirez said entering the kitchen and the conversation. He was so consumed with jealousy he had given himself a temporary fever. A few feet from the stove he stood, legs spread apart and fists clenched in rock knots like he was about to box with God.

Bradley was too drunk to hear the disdain in Ramirez's voice but Race detected her husband's envy easily. Part of her plan was to make him insanely jealous but she had no *idea it would work so easily and so quickly. She didn't even do her real work yet.*

Race figured she'd gotten her plan in motion when she switched the cooking sherry to brandy while flirting softly with Bradley but Christmas had come early for her.

Ramirez was furious!

And she loved it.

Ramirez, tinged with Scarlett's pussy juice, walked up to Race and looked down at the saucepot. Using the same digit he finger fucked Scarlett with moments earlier, he dipped it into the sauce and licked it off. "This tastes good, baby," Ramirez said to Race. "Just like you used to make."

"Man, your wife can burn," Bradley said, still slightly inebriated.

Ramirez looked at him and back at Race. "Can you tell me why this nigga talking to me like I don't know shit about my wife?"

Race did all she could to hold her laughter. "Baby, are you okay? You seem out of it?"

"Nah, I'm good," Ramirez responded.

"Me too," Bradley interjected. "Let me go upstairs and see if Denim gonna let me get into the draws before dinner. Because Race got me feeling right with that sherry."

Ramirez was five seconds from stealing his brother in the jaw, instead his teeth clenched. The last thing he wanted to hear was that Race did anything that helped stimulate his brother into wanting to fuck. Even if Bradley was referring to liquor. "Yeah...you go see about yours. I got matters down here."

When Bradley walked away Ramirez rubbed Race's shoulders. "I want us to start spending more time together, bae. I feel like we passing Bentleys in the night. Ain't no quality time being shared between us. This lock down could be the best thing for us and our marriage."

"You're right and I'm gonna work overtime to show you how much I want this. I want to do the same with the family too. Bambi, Denim and Scarlett need my time also. I can't believe it took the kidnapping for me to realize how important everyone is to me."

Ramirez removed his hands off her shoulders and crossed his arms over his chest. "Well I'm talking about me and you." He frowned.

"I'm confused," Race said.

"Family is important but I want us to get back to the way we use to be. Where you relied on me to be there for you. To be that rock for you. There will be plenty of time for a family affair later." He paused. "For now, I'm talking about building back our bond."

"I understand, Ramirez. And I'm willing to do whatever it takes to give you exactly what you deserve."

He kissed her on the lips not realizing she was frowning the whole time.

CHAPTER ELEVEN

DENIM

It seemed like everyone was giggling extra hard at the dinner table tonight and it was making me a little angry. Besides, we had a sensitive baby in the building who didn't know us yet.

Where was the respect?

As I held Master in my arms, every time someone chuckled too hard his eyes would fly open and it would take a steady rock to get him to settle down again.

They had no consideration for Master but I did. A bunch of fucking drunks they were.

The more I looked down at him the more I realized God brought him into my life, to love, to nurture and to hold. I wanted to be his mother and I was going to do a great job at it too.

When I looked up again, there seemed to be several different conversations taking place. Scarlett with Bambi and Kevin. Race and Bradley and then there was Ramirez who looked like he was five seconds from killing everyone.

Finally there was me and Master.

I focused all of my attention on him. It felt good holding him in my arms. I loved the smell of his skin, the softness of his hair and the love that seemed to spill from his eyes as he looked up at me.

I had a right to fall for him. After a few days I spent at least five hours out of the day caring for this child. Don't get me wrong, every now and again Scarlett would ask for him back but for the most part he was in my room and I think Bradley resented me for it.

I know he loved our little girl but I believe he felt like I was trying to replace her with his nephew and that wasn't the case. I was concerned that Scarlett with her reckless behavior couldn't love him properly and I was not about to let something happen to him like it did with Jasmine when she broke her leg in the tub on Scarlett's watch.

"Okay, okay, everyone," Race said standing up. She held a champagne glass in her hand and dinged the side of it twice with a fork. Everyone settled down and grew slightly quiet. "I want to say something but first everyone needs a drink."

Kevin looked at Bambi and her water glass. "I can get the cider from the fridge, baby," he said to her.

She shook her head. "No...um...I'm fine with water."

"Are you sure? Because we don't have to drink if it's uncomfortable for you," Kevin continued.

Except he was lying. Being locked down meant lots of alcohol to pass the time and she was bound to get tempted. Nobody was gonna push back on an occasional drink during this time. Not even me.

"I said I'm fine with water," she said more firmly.

Race cleared her throat. "Well raise whatever you have in your hand."

Bradley moved a little slowly as if he was about to pass out. Somewhere along the line he had way too much to drink but I didn't know when. One of the downfalls about being hunted was being forced to spend too much time with family and it had only been two days since the official lock down and already I was completely annoyed.

"I'm not fucking with you this time," Bradley said to Race. "You already got me messed up with that sherry."

"Well don't fuck with her then, nigga," Ramirez said. "Fall back and let her talk."

I caught the animosity in Ramirez's voice but I didn't know what inspired it. And then there was a knock on the door and he no longer mattered. It was as if all of the alcohol had been sucked from everyone's veins, as they all slid their weapons from underneath the table slowly reminding us that we were at war.

I put Master in the crib further away from the door and grabbed my weapon too.

Slowly, while aimed, everyone crept to the front door. Kevin and Bambi were the closest but it was Bambi who looked out of it and then back at Kevin.

"Who is it?" Kevin asked her.

"You not gonna believe this shit," Bambi responded.

"Who's at the fucking door?" Kevin yelled, I guess he was unable to wait for her answer.

"Sarah," the voice said. "Sarah Cotton. Is my daughter Denim inside?"

Everyone looked at me with a major attitude while slowly lowering their weapons. "What the fuck she doing here?" Bradley barked at me. All of a sudden he was no longer drunk. I guess anger does that to you. "I thought we agreed that we were done with that bitch. Are you crazy or something?"

"I don't know why she's here," I said scratching my scalp, my blue dreads flopping around in the process. "But...but I can go see." I moved past my family members and their hard stares as I opened the door. My mother was on the other side, a black fur coat covered her dirty black t-shirt and soot stained jeans.

Looking past her I saw our soldiers guarding the property and knew why they let her into the gates. She was my mother and they wouldn't turn her away although I wish they bothered to phone first. Still, she was on the list. We forgot to take her off after the last beef and that alone gained her entry.

I opened the door wider and my mother came inside, looked at everyone and dropped a trash bag directly on top of the taco sauce on the table. Placing her hands on her hips she said, "I don't know why ya'll staring at me like you crazy. This my family too."

Bambi sighed.

"Bitch, this not your family," Bradley barked. "I thought I told you before to find your own way."

"And I tried to do that!" My mother yelled. "But because of you all I can't live my life." She rotated her finger. "So I came here."

"What does that mean you can't live your life?" Bambi asked. "You a grown ass woman."

"Some Pakistanian looking men been coming around my house, asking about all of you." She paused, pointing long fingers at each of us. "Now I don't know what trouble you into but I'm not about to die because of it. So as far as I'm concerned the decision is easy. You have to take me in."

Kevin stepped closer to her, his fists clenched and I stood beside him in case I needed to block a blow. "Do you remember what you said to us, the last time I saw you?"

My mother waived her hand. "How could I remember what I said months ago…life moves quickly you know?"

"Well I remember everything. You said, '*I don't know what it is about you Kennedy's. Can't run an operation and can't save your own people. And tell me something, what is it about ya'll that makes you keep losing kids? First Jasmine, then Master and now the twins. Is no one safe around you fake ass gangsters?*'" He paused. "And now you show up here?"

I was shocked that Kevin remembered verbatim what her words were but then again that was a very painful night. He lost one child and a brother, and my mother was insensitive as she spilled such malicious things from her lips.

"Listen, I was an evil person when I was last here but if you allow me to come back I promise to stay out of the way. You won't hear from me at all. Trust me, I've learned my lesson."

"You can't stay here," Bradley said shaking his head from left to right. "That's out the question. Now we'll give you some money to find another place but-"

"There's no place safer in the world than right here, in the Kennedy compound, and I'm not going anywhere." She pointed at the floor. "You'll have to kill me first."

And then everyone looked at me.

I could tell they wanted me to make the decision that would send her on the way but she was my mother. Which is why I told her to lie to them about Abd asking around about us in the first place. I knew it was the only way to get them to even consider opening the front door. Because although my mother could be messy they wouldn't want to see me lose her after I'd lost so much already.

"You gonna tell her to bounce or not?" Bradley asked. "We waiting."

I looked down, around the room and back at him. "She's my mother. If she goes, I go too. Is that what you want?"

Bradley stormed off, waking the baby.

CHAPTER TWELVE

RACE

I held the phone I used to re-route the calls from the Dope Phone Scarlett was supposed to be manning against my ear. While disguising my voice I gave the men bad direction that would cause a war, which was also a part of my plan. "Yes, we are making drops next week, Thursday to be exact. Once you go to the location I just gave you, you will be given your delivery," I lied.

Rollo, who I liked the least of all our customers, which is why I selected him, sighed. "I hope you guys are coming through this time with the fruit, Scarlett. Because this beef is fucking with my operation. If this is postponed again I might have to find another distributor."

"So you think we want it like this?" I paused. "The operation gonna be up and running next week, like I said. Just meet us at that location and things will be fine."

"Yeah aight."

When I finished with the call I tucked the phone into my panty drawer, covered it with a few La Perla pieces and grabbed my other cell phone. I hadn't spoken to my New Friend all day and figured now was as good a time as any.

Lying on my bed, face up, I dialed the number and waited for his voice to come on the line. For some reason I had gotten used to speaking to him as opposed to texting so I went with what I felt. "Hey sexy," he said. "You gonna be rich because I was just thinking about you."

"I'm rich now."

"No doubt." He laughed. "I fucking love your sexy ass."

"You know that's so unfair that you know who I am but I don't know which one you are." I rolled over on my side and looked out the open bedroom door. "I'm jealous."

He chuckled. "You wanted it this way remember? I'm just keeping your plan alive. Go with the flow."

"I wish I remembered why I agreed to it."

"I think the real reason is because you like mystery. Why else wouldn't you have asked me which one I am?"

I smiled. "Yeah, maybe that's the reason, either way I don't want to ruin it. Like you said let's keep with the plan." For some reason I slipped my hand into my jeans, into my panties and against my clit. I didn't want phone sex from him but all this revenge shit had gotten me horny.

"Good, I figured you'd want it to remain this way," he paused. "So how's your plan coming on with those who betrayed you? You sound in a better mood."

I continued to rub my clit. "It's coming on too good."

"Are you excited about that?"

When I realized he wanted a real conversation I removed my fingers from my pussy and wiped the juice onto Ramirez's pillow to dry them off. "I am excited but it's making me think things are too good to be true. Like in a matter of time things will go badly."

"So what if they do? Stay with the present. Stuff is working right now and already you got the upper hand. They have no idea you're coming for them. You know how many plans I put into motion only for them to fall through? You got the advantage. Roll with it."

I sighed. "I guess the other reason I feel bad is because I don't feel bad. To make this shit work I got to get people involved that don't have anything to do with it, you know?"

"Are the people you involving getting hurt? I mean, physically?"

I sat up and leaned against the black headboard. "No...of course not."

"Well it's a necessary evil."

I laughed. "You sound like you're having more fun with my revenge games than I am. It's not that I don't like it but still you are really enjoying yourself."

He chuckled. "Listen, I just want to see you win. Your man hurt you and I want you to get the revenge you desire. What's wrong with that?"

"Who said it was my man?"

"It's always about a man."

I laughed. "Why you want to see me win so much?" I wiggled my toes and realized I needed to have them done. Since we can't leave maybe I can get Bambi to do them for me if I do hers too. I can never do my own. "You barely know me."

"I want this over so we can get to the business we have with each other."

I laughed. "And what business is that?"

"I'm gonna wait until you handle this situation with your husband before telling you everything you need to know." He paused. "Trust me, I'm a patient man."

"Race, can I talk to you for a minute?" Denim asked entering my room.

I didn't even hear her come inside.

I'm slipping.

"Uh, sure, Denim." I directed my attention to the call. "I'll...hit you back," I whispered. I nervously threw my phone down like she was my husband and had caught me red-handed.

"Who was that?" She questioned sitting next to me on the bed.

"Just a friend."

She smiled. "I'll take that as a queue to leave it alone, for now anyway." She sighed deeply and looked out into the room. "I guess you're mad at me too. About my mother."

I shook my head and positioned my body to look into her eyes. "Why, Denim? Why would you let her back when you know how she is? Think about all the sneaky shit she's done and all the manipulative games she ran on you. Why invite her into our world when she's undeserving?"

"She's all I have, Race. Bradley and I haven't been able to fuck long enough to have another child so she's the only blood relative I got on earth. And I need her safe. I wish people understood me with that part."

"And I get the need to have her safe, Denim. I totally understand that you must protect your mother but she's like gasoline and water in this house. It doesn't mesh. I mean...is she important enough to sever the bond with the family? With your husband?"

"You know that's not the case."

"So make her leave!" I pleaded.

Denim looked at me for what seemed like forever. "Like I said I can't do that." She looked down at her fingers. "I wish I understood this strange hold she has over me but I don't get it myself."

I sighed. "I do, she's your mother. I might not like it but I get all that mess. Still, it's not smart." I paused. "So you were serious about saying if she leaves you will too?"

"Very."

I shook my head several times. "Well, I'm standing by you regardless." I hugged her closely. "But before you leave I want to talk to you about something else. Keep your eye on Scarlett."

"You know I always have my eyes on that bitch. I never trusted her and I'm not about to start now."

"Good, because I don't think she's taking the best care of Master that she can. I believe in fact that I caught her giving him some type of medicine to put him to sleep the other day," I lied.

"What the fuck?" She yelled jumping up. "I'm gonna choke the fuck outta that white bitch!"

I pulled her hand down. "Denim, just listen and don't step to her about it because I'm not sure. I said I think I saw her. All I want you to do is keep an eye on her and the baby. You may even want to step up more than you have been as far as watching him more hours and all. That way we can be sure he's fine. I would do it myself but you're a mother. I've never been so I might make shit worse. Do you think you can do that?"

Denim's nostrils flared. "Of course but if she hurts that baby I'll do more than just look after him. I'll kill her! Because I don't care what you say, she had something to do with hurting Jasmine when she put her in the tub that night. I may never find out the truth but I know it in my heart, and that's enough for me."

"I got it, Denim. And you should always go with what you feel."

CHAPTER THIRTEEN

BAMBI

I was sitting in my closet on the floor going over old pictures of when times were good in my life and with my family. Back in the day when we were whole and the twins were home.

I had a half a bottle of vodka in my right hand and a glass in the left. After realizing the cup was slowing my need to get fucked up down, I tossed it on the floor and sucked right out of the bottle.

Nobody knew about the eight bottles I had hidden in my closet but me. In the past I would go to the bar and grab a drink or two but since we couldn't leave I resorted to going harder and drinking in my closet for privacy.

Looking down at the picture of my twins I realized guilt weighed on me more than I imagined. Yes I had problems with Noah but he was still my son and to wish that he would die instead of Melo had me plagued with pain.

He's gone and I can't help but feel like I wished it on him.

Soon my teardrops fell on the photos causing the paper, which held the images, to swell.

And then Kevin walked inside.

"Fuck, Bambi! I knew you were drinking again."

He caught me.

Looking down, he shook his head and sat next to me. I could see the anger on his face due to my habit getting worse but suddenly it drifted away. For that moment he became my husband, reminding me why we would always be together. I lie in his lap and cried as he stroked my hair. "Baby, I'm so sorry about all of this. You were a good girl before you started fucking with me and now you've lost a son."

"I wished Noah would die, Kevin," I sobbed. "I wished he would die and he did. How could I call myself a mother and think of something so horrible about my own child? What is wrong with me?"

"There was a lot going on, Bambi and you said something you didn't mean in the moment. If I was to persecute myself every time I said something I didn't feel I would be dead. Or insane."

I sat up and looked at his face. "You think I'm weak? Too weak to handle what's happening around me?"

"You're the strongest woman I know, Bambi. But you're also a mother. Who just lost a...a..." He shook his head and wiped his hand down his face. "A child. My only concern is that you not show weakness around the family. We need to be strong for them. Don't want folks thinking we can't handle things. We're in too much."

His shoulders hunched a little.

And it was at that time that I remembered he had lost too. It's not that I forgot he was Noah's father or Camp's brother but grief has a way of making you feel alone. I guess that's the selfishness of it all.

"The alcohol has to stop, Bambi," he said taking the bottle from me. "It only makes things worse."

"But I don't want to feel the pain right now. And alcohol is the only thing that can get me there."

"You are strong enough to deal with everything that comes your way," he continued. "Pain reminds us that we human. We might not like it but we shouldn't run from it either. If you wanna cry do it. If you want to yell do it but leave the liquor out of it and make sure your pain is in private."

"I'm not you, Kevin! And I don't want to remember the things I said in the moment about Noah! I want the hurt to stop, Kevin! Make it stop!"

He sighed. "This street you're going down is bad. You cannot handle alcohol. You know it, Bambi, it's terrible for the family and our business. You're different when you drink and I don't want that for you. I don't want that for our marriage."

"So you're saying you won't love me if I drink?"

"Yes. That's exactly what I'm saying. Because the woman who uses is not my wife. You become something else that I'm not attracted to."

Nothing hurts more than your man telling you he's not charmed by you. I realize that should be enough to put the bottle down but I'm not giving my liquor up for anyone, not even my husband.

At least right now anyway.

"Sarge's family is here," Race said standing at the closet doorway. From where she stood she looked at me with sadness and I hated when people did that. Keep your pity for yourself, was my motto.

I stood up. "I'm coming now."

Kevin rose also and Race walked away. "We have company, play your part as the queen of the house...not a drunk."

"I'm the woman of this house regardless if I drink or not." I snatched my bottle back from him and took a large swig. Liquid rolled down the sides of my face. "Remember that."

I felt a little wobbly as I walked down the hall to the living room but I remained on my feet. Once there I was shocked when I saw Sarge's family. I don't know what I assumed but I didn't expect his wife to be so young and so beautiful. Both her and her daughter looked like models and I figured they had to be gold diggers.

Their beauty was dangerous.

Don't get me wrong, Sarge is powerful and powerful men attract beautiful women but this...

His wife's complexion was the color of coffee with a tablespoon of milk. Her black hair hung in long loose soft curls around her face like a frame. Judging by the fitted red dress she chose to wear her bra size was about an A cup, her waist tiny and her hips with just the right curve.

Her daughter was the exact carbon copy, just younger and smaller.

"Thank you so much for allowing us into your home," the wife said extending her well-manicured hand my way. "My name is Believe and this is my daughter Treasure."

I shook both of their fingertips loosely before taking another swig. Their skin was soft as if they hadn't done any hard work all their lives.

"Welcome," Kevin said.

Believe looked at the bottle in my hand and it was hard to tell but I felt she was judging me in that moment. "Yes, welcome to my home. I am Bambi Kennedy."

"The pleasure will be all mine," Believe said.

"Is that right?" I responded before laughing.

Kevin cleared his throat and shook their hands also. "Sarge is loyal to my family so the least we can do is protect his by inviting you here. We hope that you are comfortable."

She smiled. "Thank you, Kevin, I intend on making myself very comfortable. Besides, I've heard so much about you both." She looked at me. "And I want you to know that Treasure and I will be a help around here until things blow over and we return home. I'm a great cook so anything you need from me I'm willing to provide." She gazed at Kevin.

He nodded his head and then looked back at me. "Well, let me show you to your room," he said.

With thoughts of my son still heavy on my mind, I walked the other way.

BELIEVE & TREASURE

After Kevin showed Believe and Treasure to their room Believe sat her Louis Vuitton bags on the floor and locked the door. Waiting for a few seconds for Kevin to walk down the hall and out of earshot, she rushed up to Treasure and they both jumped up and down excitedly in each other's arms.

"Mother, look at this place," Treasure said as she walked over to one of the two queen beds in the room. She threw her body on top of the plush mattress and looked up into the ceiling. "It's spectacular! We're actually here! In the Kennedy compound! Can you believe this? It can't be real."

Believe sauntered toward the other bed, rubbing her hand along the cool paneling of the exquisite cream design for the bedpost. She was taking in every moment. Savoring each object wishing it all belonged to her.

Slowly she sat down and Treasure popped up, both sitting across from one another. "Soon we will have the revenge that is ours. The life that is ours." Through clenched teeth she continued. "For years Sarge has pledged loyalty to this family and finally we will repay them in kind by fucking up their lives." She pointed at the floor.

Treasure got up and sat next to her mother. "Whatever you need me to do, mother, I will do."

Believe stroked her daughter's long hair. "You need not do much, not now anyway. Just be ready to fuck and suck when the time is right. The rest will be up to me."

CHAPTER FOURTEEN
RACE

We were soaking in the hot tub within our poolroom drinking wine. Mine, a golden colored Riesling. Scarlett's, a red Merlot that was laced with a little drug, courtesy of me. When she dripped some wine on her grey swimsuit I blew a small sigh of relief when I realized she didn't spill enough to fuck up my plans. She needed to drink her venom for it to work.

Not waste it on her fake tits.

"I love that red bathing suit, Race," she said. "You look really good in it."

"I try to keep it tight. Gotta make sure Ramirez likes what he sees." I winked.

She cleared her throat and looked away from me. "I'm glad we were able to do this," she said holding onto her glass before taking another large gulp. I tried to hide the pleasure brewing up inside of me, because I knew within an hour she would be three sheets to the wind. "It doesn't happen enough between us. This alone time."

"Well I'm glad we are able to do it now," I replied. "If there's anything to be said about this lock down connecting with family is it. I just want you to know I haven't made time for you in the past but now you will have all of my attention. Trust me."

Scarlett waved the air, her eyes already seeming a little lower than before. "I understand how things are, you have a lot on your plate with helping...helping...Bambi and all. At least...at least...we have....now."

"Are you okay?" I questioned. "You seem out of it."

"Uh...yes...well...maybe I had too much wine." She paused, touching her forehead. "It's been a long time since I tore down half a bottle." She giggled. "Probably was way too much."

I stood up, removed the glass from her hand and placed it on the side of the hot tub. "Let me help you to your room. The last thing you need to do is fall asleep in here and drown." I frowned.

Although that would've been perfectly okay with me.

"Yes...yes...maybe you're right, Race."

Now she was knocked out, naked.

Lying on top of her bed.

The final thing she did when she got into the room was remove her bathing suit allowing me to get a good look at the body that kept my husband's dick company. The plan was to slip her into her purple pajamas but the drug I placed into her bottle was so potent it wouldn't allow for such a small act.

There was no way she could dress herself.

So I gazed at her as long as I wanted.

Standing over her bed I focused on her pale flesh, way brighter than her black comforter. Her nipples, the color of ginger and cream. Suddenly I wanted to touch her to see what he felt when he ran his fingertips over her protruding breasts.

First I started with her face. Warm to the touch but slightly clammy due to her body overheating while trying to fight the temporary poison that consumed her bloodstream. Slowly my finger ran across her thin lips before finding it onto the floor of her pink tongue.

He probably liked his dick there most of all.

Inside of her mouth he could forget the vow he made to me while pressing his stick in and out of this hot area before releasing his fluids down her throat.

How does it feel? I pressed one finger inside her mouth. The second finger and followed it up with a third.

She probably even swallows. I frowned. She looks like the type.

I hate this bitch.

Sliding my fingers out of her mouth I touched her neck. It was thin and delicate like a fragile piece of porcelain. Using two hands I massaged her throat and played with the idea of choking her to death. However, I let the plan go realizing killing her would be too easy.

I already discussed this with my New Friend. So why did I keep bringing it up? Death was not a possibility and needed to be forgotten. Total destruction of their worlds with me as the silent coach was my plan so I had to stick to detail.

Still, I got wet thinking about squeezing the life out of her right now. There was a soft hint of power knowing that if I did commit the crime nobody would think it was me. They would be liable to blame Sarah or Sarge's family before they ever looked my way.

A perk of having strangers in the home I guess.

Tiring of her neck I ran my fingers over her right breast.

And then the left.

I could barely feel the implants she paid for and knew Ramirez enjoyed them too. Just a mouthful is all I need. Yours are perfect is what he told me when I considered doing it myself. I bet he didn't have a problem with fake tits now.

Down her sternum and along her belly, I continued to trace her body with my fingertips.

And then I stopped abruptly, right before I got to her pussy.

Her hairless entry.

That cave that threatened to ruin my marriage.

Frowning, I pushed her legs apart and stuck one finger inside of her first, then the second, and then the third and fourth. She felt gooey inside. Now, using my fist, I tried my best to slam her uterus into her belly. Unable to get aroused she was dry and tomorrow I knew she would be in excruciating pain.

Still, she'd never blame me but Ramirez would probably be another question. After all, he'd fucked her before why not do it while she's sleep?

When I was done putting her in pain, I wiped her pussy juice on the bed and stared down at her. "You will pay for coming into my world, Scarlett. I will take everything you love. Get ready for the ride."

Knock. Knock. Knock.

I turned around and focused on the door with wide eyes.

Not wanting to be looked at like a freak I covered her naked, unconscious body with her sheet and walked toward the sound. Before opening it I took a deep breath and slowly pulled it to me.

Denim was holding Master and I positioned myself so she could not see into the room. "Oh, I didn't know you were here, Race." She said. "She told me to bring him back at this time although I don't know why. I could've kept him longer."

I took him from her arms. "Well, he's her baby," I whispered. "Just make sure you come back here and get him later in the morning."

"No doubt." She looked at her watch. "Is she up? It's three o'clock in the morning."

"Yes, in the bathroom."

She nodded. "Well like you said I'll be back later in the AM to get him again. He's been bathed and fed and is definitely ready for sleep."

"Okay, see you soon, Denim."

She walked away and I softly closed the door. Scarlett hadn't moved an inch. I took a second to look at Master and smiled. It would be a different night for the kid but I'm sure he could handle it. After all, he's a Kennedy.

The plan? Instead of taking him to his bed I would be placing him in the tub.

Except it wouldn't be me. His mother would be to blame.

When Denim came back in the morning they would go off on Scarlett.

And I would sit back and watch this house erupt with drama.

CHAPTER FIFTEEN

DENIM

My mother was sitting on the edge of my bed when I woke up from a brief nap. I rubbed my eyes, looked around the room frantically for Bradley and back at her. Scooting closer I said, "What you doing in here, ma? Where's Bradley? He's gonna kill you."

"Who cares where that nigga is?" She shrugged. "I swear I don't know why you put up with that good for nothing man of yours anyway. He seems like more of a problem than a help. Not even as fine as the other Kennedy's if you ask me."

"Nobody's asking you!" I sighed. "Mother, you have to be careful about the liberties you been taking around here. People don't want you in this house. It's bad enough I had to let you borrow that lie to convince them to let you stay. Don't fuck it up for the both of us by being extra as fuck!"

She rolled her eyes and breathed deeply before exhaling. I could smell the garlic on her breath and figured she'd been in the kitchen helping herself as usual. "I can tell you cooked something to eat. Please say you cleaned up behind yourself."

She frowned. "So you don't have staff in this big ass house no more? The last time I was here—"

"No, ma, we don't have staff in this big ass house! We had to reduce the number of people who live here because we can hardly trust anybody." I moved closer. "Do you understand? This is a really sensitive time for this family. We don't need anybody antagonizing us. And that means you too."

She frowned. "*Antagonizing* us? If that's what you feel I'll just leave, Denim. I mean, it's obvious you don't want me here! That's one thing I'm certain of just by the tone of your voice." She waved her hand in my face but remained seated. "After all, I'm just this amazing burden."

"I never said that."

"Then why is it that the slightest thing I do warrants a threat for you to throw me out? Would you want to live under the constant danger of being homeless? Because say what you want, I always provided a place for you and Grainger to live. Forgive me if all I'm asking is to not be alone and for you to do the same for me. You're my only living child!"

I wiped my hand down my face. "You're right, ma. I'm sorry. I just —"

Bradley walked into the room and his eyes widened. "Fuck you doing in here, Sarah?"

I stood up, hoping to block some of the rage he had coming her way. "She was stopping by to ask if we wanted anything for breakfast. So everything's cool, Bradley." I put my palms on his chest. "She was just leaving."

"No I didn't come in here to ask this nigga if he wanted something to eat," My mother said. "He fucking my daughter, the least he could do is cook for me." She laughed. "Besides, he knows damn well I wouldn't fix a plate for him I wouldn't spit in first."

"You see what I'm saying?" he said pointing at her but looking at me. "This is the woman who's gonna be the death of our marriage. You sure you wanna do this?"

"Ma, why would you say that to him? Tell him you didn't mean it."

"Oh, hush, Denim, I'm going to my room now. I was just coming in to say hello but if it caused all this drama never mind." She walked past Bradley, bumping into him on her way out the door.

"Is she worth our marriage, Denim?" he asked pointing in the direction she went before moving closer to me. "I need to know right now!"

"What? Of course not!"

"Are you sure about that? Because you don't listen to me when I say she's bad for our relationship. I'm not about to be with a woman who doesn't obey me and trust my leadership!" He continued.

"Bradley, I do everything you ask. Everything! I hardly ever go against you except this once. She is my mother and I—"

"You know what, fuck this shit!"

He stormed out and I threw myself on the bed. I was in a tough position because sometimes I believed my mother was in a power struggle with my husband. On purpose. Like she was actually trying to sabotage my shit. All of her men had left for one reason or another and Bradley had always remained at my side, loving me no matter what we'd gone through.

Could she be jealous?

Maybe she resented the relationship we had and was doing her best to poke holes into it. But how could I prove she didn't just miss me and was acting out? Right now she was all talk and there was nothing firm to stand on. Maybe it was best to leave her alone.

Suddenly I heard some yelling in the house.

Since I wasn't completely dressed I grabbed my robe and rushed toward the sound that appeared to be coming from Scarlett's room upstairs. Worried, I trotted up the steps only to see Bambi holding Master and yelling at Scarlett at the top of her lungs.

"Why would he be in the fucking tub, Scarlett?" Bambi continued, as Scarlett stood before her with her hands on the sides of her face. "You mean to tell me you couldn't hear this baby crying?"

"I don't know...I...can't remember putting him in there." She rubbed her temples. "I mean why would I do that? It doesn't make any sense."

"In the tub?" I asked coming inside. "What's going on?" I took Master from Bambi's arms and checked his body quickly. He seemed to be okay.

Bambi sighed, her breath smelling like liquor. "I came by earlier to ask Scarlett about the calls and I heard Master crying in the bathroom," she said to me. "I don't know if she was about to give him a bath and forgot or what."

My eyes widened as I focused back on the monster across the room. "Fuck is wrong with you, Scarlett?" I said charging her. I wanted to wrap my hands around her throat but Bambi stopped me and I had Master in my other arm.

"I talked to her about it already, Scarlett. No need in—"

"There you go taking up for her again," I pointed out. "When you gonna realize that your perfect princess is capable of doing wrong?"

"It's not about that!" Bambi yelled. "I'm not gonna gang up on her with you when I already addressed the issue."

I rolled my eyes. "You know what, I don't even care. All I know is that from here on out Master will be staying with me," I said to Scarlett. "And if you're right in the head and only if you're right in the head, I'll allow you visitation, Scarlett." I stormed off, with my child in my arms.

CHAPTER SIXTEEN

DENIM

"What's wrong, Master?" I said as I looked down at him with love and confusion. "Are you sick? Because you can't be hungry. You just ate."

He was uneasy as he lie in my arms and nothing I did seemed to calm him down. Maybe it was the fight a minute ago that put him on edge. I tried to rock him to sleep but he grew louder in his cries. I tried to rub his head and that seemed to frustrate him even more. Then I made small circular motions on his belly and he threw up. He was anxious and his mood made me feel unworthy. Maybe I wasn't as good a mother as I claimed.

"What can I do for you, Master?" I asked looking into his face that was flooded with tears. "What's wrong?"

I hummed for five minutes and although his eyes would widen and he would simmer within seconds he would start up again. I wanted him to love me like Jasmine and I knew if he spent more time with me then he would. He would come to care about me like I was his mother.

At least I hoped.

So I removed my breast.

Slowly I eased my nipple toward his lips and immediately his tiny hands latched onto each side as he suckled hard. I was not producing milk but the action seemed to relax him because his eyes lowered and he calmed down. Adding in a few more soft rocks and suddenly he was sound asleep in my arms.

"That's it my sweet, baby. You are mine and I don't care what anybody says. If someone tries to take you from me I will hurt them. Do you hear me, Master? I will kill them."

"What are you doing, Denim?" My mother asked as she looked at Master suckling my breast and then back at me. She closed the door behind herself. "I asked what the fuck are you doing with that child? You haven't been pregnant in years so you can't be producing milk."

"Be quiet, mother, you'll wake him again." I stood up and placed him on the other side of my bed belly down. Then I pulled the covers over his chin and paced a few areas in front of the mirror. I didn't know what to say to her because she probably would never understand.

"Denim, I'm waiting for an answer."

"He...he wouldn't sleep, mother. I think he had a long night because Scarlett put him in the tub and he was tired. All I was doing was trying to relax him so he could get some rest."

She walked deeper into my room. "So you gave him your titty to suck on? What kind of weirdness is that?"

My chin dipped downward. "Ma, what do you want?" I crossed my arms over my chest. "You know you're not supposed to be in here. We talked about it before and yet you continue to break the rules." I walked over to the bed when I heard Master coo and pat his back softly.

He drifted back to sleep.

She sighed. "How are you, Denim?"

I looked at her and frowned. "You never asked how I was before. Ever. So why start now? I mean, don't make this into a bigger situation than it is. This baby is an emotional wreck and I'm giving him the love he needs." I pointed at him. "Stay out of it."

"Denim, you haven't had a chance to properly grieve for Jasmine. On the surface you look strong but now..." she looked at Master. "Now I'm not so sure things are going as well as I thought."

I moved closer and in a thick whisper said, "How the fuck you gonna come in my room and tell me about my daughter? Huh?" I pushed her shoulder and she backed away. "You never once asked how I was doing when she died. The only thing you were concerned with was how much money I could give you. Or what I could do for you. And now you want to play mother of the year?"

"I never attempted to get an award for being a good mother but it doesn't mean I don't care." She pointed at me. "And I'm asking you now. How are you holding up because I don't like what I'm seeing?"

"No," I said shaking my head. "I won't allow you to play mother right now so you'll feel better about yourself in the future. If you ask me you are my child and you won't stand in my room and question me in my home! I don't owe you shit, not even an explanation."

"You had your nipple in a baby's mouth who is not yours." She paused. "Now when I say you haven't dealt with losing Jasmine that's exactly what I mean. And nothing you can say will change that."

I stormed to the door, held the knob and pointed toward the hallway. "Get out, ma. I'm not doing this with you right now."

She didn't move.

"Get the fuck out before I throw you out of my house!" I yelled.

Master started crying. "Now look what you've done. You've awakened my baby. My precious baby."

Slowly my mother moved toward the exit, dusting her beefy knees with the pale part of her hands. Taking a deep breath she said, "You are crazier than I thought. But let me leave you alone as you requested. Guess you 'bout to give him your titty again. Freak." She stormed out and I slammed the door behind her.

And now it was me who regretted that she was staying here.

BRADLEY

The weather was perfect. Not too hot and not too cold as Bradley sat on the back porch. Armed men surrounded the yard, their backs in his direction as they focused on the horizon, to ensure no one would storm the compound with the Kennedy's in their sights. Holding a can of beer in his hand he took a sip as Race walked out and brought him another.

He accepted the can, looked up at her and smiled. "You gonna get me in trouble with all of this liquor and shit. What you need, a new drinking partner or something?" He chuckled.

She sat next to him. "I've been told I'm a bad influence but I'm a little selfish today because I could use the company. I hope you don't mind."

"Why would I mind?" He sighed. "I could use the company too." Bradley finished off his first beer and opened the second. Taking a sip he looked over at her. "Do you realize you and I hardly ever spend any time together? All of these years and unless it's in a family function we don't connect. Why you think that is?"

She shrugged. "Not sure why. Maybe life moves so quickly and this family is so huge that — "

"I never realized how cool you were," he said interrupting her. "I really enjoy spending time with you. You easygoing."

She smiled. "Thank you...I think."

Bradley faced the yard and sighed. "Have you talked to Denim? I mean really talked to her?"

Race took a deep breath. "Yes, of course. She's my friend."

"Then what's wrong with her? Why the fuck would she let her mother come in here and ruin what we got? And if

it's not Sarah it's Master. It's like she's losing it now. She's not my wife anymore and I don't know what to do, Race."

"I'm sure she said this to you repeatedly but it's the truth. Sarah's her mother and she can't have anything happen to — "

"I'm falling out of love with her, Race. I'm starting not to care about her anymore and I don't want that for us. I made her my wife for life but now I'm feeling like it was a mistake."

Race shuffled a little upon hearing his cold words. It wasn't just what he said but how he said it that gave her chills. She wanted to make Ramirez jealous by spending time with Bradley but divorcing her friend was too heavy a conversation, even if she needed to get close to him. "Bradley, I'm gonna need you to never talk to me about that kind of thing again. Okay?"

He sighed.

"She's my friend, first and always," Race continued. "Can you understand and respect that?"

He handed her the beer and walked away.

CHAPTER SEVENTEEN

RAMIREZ

L *aying in the dark on a bed in the only empty guest room available in the house, Ramirez nodded his head as he listened to old school music on the radio. He fired up a blunt, pulled on it and allowed the sweet smoke to fill his lungs. He felt alone in the house because although Race promised to work on their marriage it was like she was all talk and no show. Sure, she let him fuck her a few times from the back and suck her titties but if he was being honest it was like he was sleeping with a mannequin.*

She wasn't into it at all.

He knew he lost her and that fucked with his head. He wanted his wife but he wanted her in the way he did. He preferred her submissive and mousy like she was back in the day but that wasn't Race anymore.

So what could he do?

Divorce was not an option. He would kill her before seeing another man with her.

He was so confused, his ego swelling by the thought.

And then Scarlett walked inside closing and locking the door behind herself.

Eager to submit.

He frowned. "What you doing here?" He took a pull of the weed, sending puff clouds in the air. "I didn't send for you."

"Well I've been looking for you. You weren't at dinner and you weren't at breakfast this morning." She inhaled deeply. "If you wasn't ignoring everybody I would start taking it personally."

He laughed but gave no response.

She sighed. "So you been in here all day smoking?" She looked around.

"What you want, Scarlett? Because I'm tired of acting like I'm some black nigga lusting after a white woman in my own house." He pointed at the floor. "Either you want to fuck me or you don't. There's not a lot to it and to tell you the truth I don't care anymore."

She smiled and moved closer, sitting in the only chair in the room. "Did you have sex with me the other day? When I was sleep? The night I left Master in the tub?"

"Did you really do that? With my nephew?"

"I can't remember putting him there. It makes no sense."

He frowned. "No...I didn't have sex with you. And why you ask me that anyway?"

"Because I was sore down there. Between my legs."

He laughed. "So let me guess, you 'bout to say I raped you next? Classic shit." He shook his head.

"Ramirez!"

He sat up "I asked what you want, Scarlett? I'm not playing games with you no more. Sex is all I can offer and you can either deal with it or not. What I won't do is play mental games with you. I got a wife for that already."

She frowned. "I never asked you for anything more than what we had."

"Then why the games?"

She got up and walked closer to the bed in the dark before dropping the red robe she was wearing. The moonlight from the cracked window shined against her vanilla colored skin and her strawberry colored hair fell over her shoulders. He couldn't help but grin. She was perfect.

He pressed the blunt out in the ashtray next to the bed and sat on its edge, his feet brushing the floor. "Are you gonna fuck me or what, Scarlett?"

Ramirez released his dick from his pants and stroked until he was stiff as she watched, licking her lips. "We can do whatever you want."

"Then come get this dick."

"Yes, sir…"

Scarlett moved closer, crawled on top of him and lowered her body until her pussy engulfed his warmth. In ecstasy, and loving how she felt, he held the sides of her waist and pumped in and out of her as he looked into her eyes. This is *how he liked his women, submissive and weak. If only Race would fall in line he wouldn't have to beat up Scarlett's pussy.* "Why you make me wait, huh? You know I been wanting to fuck you again."

"I'm sorry. From here on out I won't fight you, Ramirez." *She said.* "We do what we do and we'll worry about the consequences later." *Feeling his dick pulsating, before he came, she got up, dropped to her knees and locked her tongue around his dick. Looking up at him she sucked it as if her life depended on it.*

"FUCK! Right there, Scarlett, suck that dick you sexy white bitch."

Willing to obey, she jerked and sucked until his sweet cum exploded into her mouth and rolled down her throat.

They fucked twice before he finally left the room.

Completely satisfied.

Race walked into the poolroom where Bradley was sitting soaking in the hot tub. She was carrying an MCM bag with a bottle of wine and two glasses wrapped in paper towels to protect them from crashing against one another.

He was alone.

And she was relieved because she needed the private time with him.

Slowly she eased inside the hot water and sat across from him. "I'm sorry, Bradley, about earlier. I judged without even hearing you out and I should not have done that. Guess I got into my feelings and all. Since she's my friend. But can you forgive me?"

He looked away from her. "It's cool."

"No it's not." She got up and sat closer, their legs touched a little. "Staying in this house without being able to leave has driven all of us mad and I just wanted to...to..."

"Stay loyal to your friend." He looked at her and nodded. "Nothing wrong with that. I guess I figured we'd been spending so much time together that I could be real with you. Maybe I should've gone to one of my brothers instead."

"No, I want you to come to me. It was a mistake on my part and I won't shoot you down like that again." She reached into her bag and removed the bottle of wine. "I brought a peace offering if you down for it. I'm also willing to listen if you want to talk."

He chuckled. "So you bribing me now?"

She shrugged. "Is it working yet? We can't make liquor runs since we're being hunted so this bottle is worth a lot around here. Consider me the plug." She reached inside her

By **T. Styles**

bag, grabbed the glasses and poured them both some wine. "So, talk to your new best friend."

He took a sip. "So that's what we are now?"

"You don't like the term? I mean, if we gonna be new best friends the least we can do is be real with each other."

"Real is sometimes hard for people to handle."

"Well let me ask a question I always wanted to know." She paused. "Did you really try and kill Bambi over the Grainger shit?"

He frowned. "Why would you bring up that?" He wiped the water out of his eyes. "I thought we were chilling. You sure know how to fuck up a good mood."

"Didn't you get at me earlier for judging? I figured since we are cool we could talk about everything. All I want is an answer, Bradley."

He put the glass down and sighed. "I was in a fucked up state of mind and I'm not happy about what I did to her. A lot of things happened and I was afraid I would lose my wife. So I was willing to do whatever I could to prevent that from happening including silencing Bambi. For life."

As they continued to talk, Ramirez entered the poolroom holding a large towel and a major attitude when he saw the scene. They didn't know he was there yet because they were engulfed in conversation.

After fucking Scarlett he wanted to take a quick soak only to see his brother and his wife keeping more time. He took a moment to observe them before moving closer in extreme rage. "Why is it whenever I pop up I see you two niggas huddled together?" Ramirez questioned. "Race, bounce. I want some alone time with my brother for a change."

Race rose, grabbed her towel and wrapped it around her body. "I'll see you later, Bradley." She said to be irritating.

"Not if I kill this nigga first," Ramirez said through clenched teeth. "I'll be in the room later."

She grinned and walked out.

Ramirez eased into the hot tub and sat across from his brother. "At first I thought I was seeing things but now I'm certain, you got a thing for my wife, man. Don't you?"

Bradley frowned. "I know you not fucking serious."

"Do you got a thing for my wife or not, nigga? You might as well be real because it's definitely obvious! Wherever she is you are too. I mean where your wife, bruh? How come you always with mine?"

Bradley picked up his glass, took a sip of wine and leaned back. "If you so concerned about what we doing that must mean you got something going on out in the world." He pointed at him. "I mean, only a guilty man would question is brother like you do me. So come clean, bruh, what broad got your mind so fucked up that you would come at me in an unnatural way about Race?"

"Let me be clear with you, nigga, I want you to stay the fuck away from her! If I see you around her again I might be liable to hurt you. That's real, man. It's not a joke so take heed." He got out of the hot tub and stormed out.

Bradley took a sip of wine again. "Damn, this nigga really ready to kill his own blood for her. Suddenly I'm more interested."

CHAPTER EIGHTEEN

KEVIN

*K*evin walked into his bedroom looking for Bambi, only to smell a foul odor coming from inside. When he saw his wife sprawled out on the floor, he rushed to her aid hoping she was alive. Vomit covered her mouth and clothing and he quickly disrobed her before giving her a warm bath.

It took two hours for her to wake up and although love had him care for her, disgust made him hate her for it. "What you doing, Bambi?" He asked sitting next to her in the bed. "What you fucking doing to yourself? And to me? We got company in this house and you acting like a wino! I can't keep going through this shit every time you got a problem in life."

A headache threatened any peace she would have for the day so she stroked her temples and tried to relieve some pressure. "What do you want me to say? I had a little too much but I'm fine."

He frowned. "A little too much? You were on the floor passed out, Bambi! You messy as fuck in here right now and not fitting to hold my name. I'm embarrassed to even know you."

Her eyes widened. "Not fitting to hold your name? Nigga, I got bodies behind showing my love for you and your name. And now after one episode you threatening my ring?"

"You and me both know you took them bodies because you loved it." He pointed at her. "True, in the beginning you wanted no parts of the dope game but you all in now and everybody in this house know it. Now are you gonna get yourself together or not?"

"I'm having a hard time right now, Kevin." She ran her hand down her face. "Can't you understand that? And I — "

"Stop making fucking excuses! I'm convinced that you only say shit you think I wanna hear. When you get better we gotta talk about us." He stood up and looked upon her as if he wanted to spit in her face. "Because right now this not working for me and it got me rethinking the future." Kevin stormed out of the room.

Needing some peace, Kevin retreated in the only free guest room in the house. He was irritated when he smelled the weed odor stemming from it because he was trying to quit and figured Denim or Ramirez had been inside since *they smoked more than anybody. But now that the sweet aroma filled his nostrils he wanted to fire up himself.*

Instead, he flopped on the messy bed, one arm behind his head the other on his chest. He loved Bambi more than any woman had come close but he couldn't take another alcoholic episode in his life. Because contrary to what Bambi believed he was dealing with the loss of his son and brother too. Most moments he put on a front for his family but he felt like he was dying inside.

When was he going to get his moment to reflect?

"I'm sorry," Believe said entering his space. "I...I knew this was the only free room in the house and I wanted to catch some alone time. My daughter has been asking so many questions about why we're living here that I needed to think about everything before I talked to her."

Kevin popped up. "Oh, no problem. Come inside. I can go to my room. I was just thinking that's all."

He was almost at the door and she said, "Kevin, can I ask you something? I know it's personal but I need someone to turn to. I mean, I tried to call Sarge but...well you know how it is. He's been in the field working for you and is inaccessible to me. I guess I should be used to it but I never am."

He stopped, spun around and looked around the room. It was difficult staring into her beauty and he didn't want to do anything disrespectful by gazing too long. Besides, had someone did the same to his wife he would murder them quickly. "Sure, what is it?"

"You have children and I guess I'm trying to figure out...how do you...how do you deal with a traumatic experience and raise a child at the same time? Treasure is eighteen but she's never not been with Sarge and me. She's never not been in our home. What can I do to make her comfortable? To make her feel safe?"

He sighed. "You asking the wrong man."

"Maybe you're right. I'm sorry, I didn't mean to pry," she said sheepishly. "I'll let you be alone." She turned to walk away.

"Believe." She stopped and looked at him. "You aren't prying," he continued. "I'm saying that you're asking the wrong man because I haven't had any luck with raising my boys. One of my sons was killed and the other is away at college, barely talking to me or Bambi."

"That's right, I'm so insensitive. You did lose a child and here I am asking you about mine."

"Don't worry about it."

"I don't know what to do, Kevin. I feel all alone." She moved closer to him and now he could smell the vanilla lotion on her skin. "I wish...I wish Sarge was here because then I could ask him to hold me but he's not." She looked at the floor. "And...I need someone to hold me. Can you do that? If only for a minute?" Now she was staring seductively into his eyes.

Silence.

Kevin took a few steps backward. It had been along time since he had been delivered pussy on the doorstep and he had to be careful before unwrapping such an alluring gift. For all he knew this could be a set up.

But how?

And why?

She was Sarge's wife and he was certain he'd never solicit her to seduce him. Besides, what would be the benefit? Getting cut off? Still, things felt off. He made a decision, he had to leave. "I know things will work their way out. Let me go to my — "

He tried to walk away but she grabbed his hand with her butter soft fingertips. "Kevin, can you hug me? Please? I won't bother you anymore afterwards. I just want to be held for a moment or else I'm gonna break down. I'm begging you. Do you want me on my knees? Because I will just to be held."

Kevin took his time responding, considering her beauty in the process. It was as if an hour passed as he battled with where hugging her would lead. His mind told him some good pussy but still...

He was a dope boy and he knew firsthand where these types of situations ended up...trouble.

He was in his family home.

His wife with a military background, who had been trained to kill, was upstairs and still his dick was rock hard.

If he turned around to leave there would be no crime. But if he stayed he was certain that he would be amongst the guilty, diving into all kinds of danger.

And then he thought about Bambi. Drunk, upstairs and smelling like vomit. As far as he was concerned she should've been on her game knowing a beautiful woman was in their home.

But she wasn't so he would go for his.

"Sure...I can hold you for a moment," he said. "Don't see a problem with that."

That moment was more like a second before she wrapped her arms around him. Pretty soon her lips met his, maybe they needed to be held too. Quickly things escalated. The sweet kiss that felt innocent and passionate at first moved to her warm body being pressed against his as he lifted her off her feet, walked her to the bed and released his dick.

She felt better than he imagined.

But before he could press into her good, Treasure came into the room and softly kissed his back. "Fuck is this?" he asked, preparing to stop everything until Believe held his face into her soft hands and looked into his eyes. His instincts said it was a setup but the emotional rollercoaster he'd been on left him woozy.

"Roll with it, Kevin," Believe said seductively. "All I want to do is thank you for letting us stay here. Can I do that for you? I promise you're about to have the time of your life."

Treasure continued to kiss his back before her small fingers gave him a strong massage as he pushed into Believe. Wanting to do more Treasure eased on the bed, waist next to Believe's head as she opened her legs. Having a feeling that Kevin was a pussy eater, she spread her lips and sure enough he licked and sucked her sweet smelling box as he pounded into Believe.

He fucked a few bitches at the same time before but this was the first time he felt pure lust. Wanting to change shit up just a little, to experience every moment, he eased on the bed, as Treasure got on all fours. With her pussy opened Kevin pounded her from behind as Believe got under them and sucked his dick as it entered and left her daughter's body.

The creepiness of them being related mixed with the danger of Bambi being upstairs drove him crazy. The duo fucked and sucked for over an hour until Kevin exploded his cum onto Treasure's chest and watched Believe lick it off.

By **T. Styles**   177

CHAPTER NINETEEN

RACE

I just finished fielding a few more calls in Scarlett's name when Bradley came into the door. "Where's Ramirez?" I sighed in irritation because I knew where he was, probably somewhere fucking Scarlett.

"Not sure where he is nor do I care." I shrugged. "But how you two doing? After the hot tub he didn't seem too happy about us spending time together."

He sighed. "He's a funny guy." He chuckled. "My brother acting crazy as fuck but I'm not about to play into his shit either. I should be asking how you both are. Why would he think we would go there with each other?"

I cleared my throat. "Who knows what's in his head? I would've thought you got an answer from him."

"Well it doesn't bother me if it doesn't bother you." He looked into my eyes.

I walked closer. "It doesn't. I'm gonna do what I want to…always."

"Is that right?" He grinned.

"Yes." I smiled back.

"I mean how he think I would ever fuck his wife?" He looked at me for what seemed like an eternity before staring at the carpet. "That would be wrong on all types of levels."

"I don't know. Maybe it's the fact that we can't go anywhere. Boredom and isolation makes people go crazy."

"Right, but we have more luxuries here than most niggas can imagine. A poolroom, an entertainment room downstairs. It ain't like we fucked up in here."

I shrugged. "It's not always about the money. Maybe peace of mind is worth more, and in that area the Kennedy's are dead broke."

"You right about that." He looked into my eyes again. "So what you doing?"

"Nothing. Why? You gonna take me to the movies or something?"

"Yes." He chuckled. "What you want to see? That new Will Smith joint?

"Stop getting me excited." I waved the air. "You know we can't leave the house, Bradley. Abd would blow up the theater trying to get at us."

He smiled. "So you forgot about the movie room already?"

I giggled. "Actually I did. I hardly ever go down there."

"I'm there all the time. If you hung out with me in the past you would know." He winked. "Well I picked a few of my old favorites and was wondering if you would join me. I mean if you aren't doing anything."

When I looked down I saw he was holding the DVD's. I didn't know he had them in his hand before that moment. "Yeah...sure but um...where's Denim?"

"She's with Master and Sarah, in my room." He frowned. "So you coming with me or what?"

I giggled. "I don't know your movie taste but..."

"Girl, my movie taste's like that. Brace yourself because you're about to be in love with me for life behind my DVD game."

My eyes widened.

"I'm just playing...I...I...about the love thing, Race."

"Don't be so serious, Bradley. We past that now. If you can't joke with me then who else?"

"I knew you were cool," he said. "So what we waiting on, Race?"

Somehow his questioned seemed like it had two meanings but I followed him anyway.

Besides, what did I have to lose?

We were on our second bottle of vodka and I have to admit that I hadn't laughed so hard in months. This wasn't part of the plan to spend so much time with him and love it. Being with him felt too good. Bradley pulled out the movies *Friday*, *Life* and *Harlem Nig*hts and I was in heaven. It was like I never saw them and I realized I never really paid attention. Sure I sat down to watch them but something was always happening in the background that stole my attention.

Life was just about to go off and the credits were rolling when he looked at me and said, "As hard as you're laughing you must be enjoying yourself."

"You know, this is the first time I actually sat down and watched these movies and I'm so glad you invited me, Bradley. And that you took the time to pull these out your stash."

He looked at me harder and I felt he was about to do something not in the plan. And he did. Suddenly he moved in to kiss me and I backed up. With my palms faced him I said, "Bradley, we can't...we can't do this.

I'm sorry if I gave you the wrong impression but this is not what I wanted for us."

Silence.

It was one thing to play him close and flirt a little to get Ramirez angry but a whole 'nother thing to actually have sex. "I'm going back to my room." I grabbed my pillow and stood up to leave. "I'll see you—"

"It was two of them," he said gazing at the credits rolling on the movie screen. "One of them held me down while the other...while the other..." He swallowed. "At first I didn't think it was happening. I heard of shit like that going down with niggas but I was a made man. I was a Kennedy and fucking with me could get them killed." He looked at me with cold eyes. "Which it did because six months later I came back for blood. Still that was after the fact. They raped me. It turned out that's why they wanted me all along, because of my name. I was a target."

I sat down.

He had my undivided attention now.

"When I came home, I didn't know how to deal with life, Race. I...they..."

I put my hand on top of his. His skin was cold as if the life was draining from him as he was telling me this story. "You don't have to—"

"I want to talk to you about it, Race. Because…because this shit been sitting on my heart for a long time." He looked at me. "I'm a man. And that one night made me question who I really was. Who I really am. I can't even fuck my wife behind it and I don't know why."

It seemed like he wanted to go deeper and I wasn't sure if I could be there for him in that way. Still, this explains everything. The mood swings when he came home and how he tried to kill Bambi. Not to mention the fights with Denim. No wonder why he moved differently. He'd been violated in the worst way a man could. "Bradley, I'm so sorry."

"Don't say that." His neck corded. "Never feel sorry for me."

"Then what can I do?" I paused. "I mean, did you tell, Denim?"

"No…you're the only one I told. And I don't know why I revealed all this to you…except that being with you is so easy."

I looked into his eyes and this time I didn't look away. Something was happening between us that I wasn't prepared for or could deny. Suddenly I wanted to kiss him and to be there for him. Kinda like

By **T. Styles**   183

returning the favor. Not just because he wanted me but also because I desired to.

So I eased on top of him, looked down into his eyes and kissed him passionately. For five minutes our lips locked and I couldn't get over how soft his lips were. How strong his fingers felt as they traced along my back. Since we were straddling I could feel his dick getting stiffer and I wanted him deep inside of me.

"Let me feel you, Race," he said softly. "Please."

I kissed him again and suddenly his stiff dick was inside of me. He was bigger than Ramirez but my body warmed to him within seconds. Like candle wax to fire slowly I melted into his flesh.

I was home in his arms.

With him inside of me.

How is this possible?

Before long we were fucking passionately in the movie room and I was in ecstasy.

Is this what Scarlett and Ramirez felt?

CHAPTER TWENTY
BELIEVE & TREASURE

B *elieve stood in front of the mirror brushing her long hair while Treasure stood next to her doing the same, imitating her every move. "He seemed to like you a lot," Believe said proudly to her daughter. "That means you're using more of the skills I taught you. When you finally get a husband you won't be able to keep him away from you. And that's the goal to keep the money rolling in."*

Treasure smiled and placed her gold chain around her neck that had a small heart dangling at the crease of her breasts. "So what now, mother?"

"Well, tonight I want you to go to him alone and serve him again. The next day it will be all me. Together we will have him wrapped around our diamond iced fingers."

"Mother, I can't believe how much fun I had." Treasure said grinning as she walked over to the edge of her bed and flopped down. She grabbed the pink pillow on the bed, held it to her heart and smiled. "I can see why Bambi likes him so much. He's perfect in every way. Did you see his face? I loved looking at — "

Believe turned around, rushed up to Treasure and smacked her so hard her neck twisted. "Why are we doing this?" When Treasure didn't respond she grew louder. "Why we fucking doing all of this? Why are we in this house?" Whenever Believe yelled she looked like a monster and this always scared the fuck out of Treasure.

She had to answer carefully.

Holding the side of her face she searched her mind and said, "We're doing this to get revenge for what Bambi did to our family. We are here to make her pay."

"Exactly! It is not your place to guess what Bambi sees in him. It's not your place to enjoy him either. He is nothing more than bait in the scheme of things and you must always remember it less you will lose your mind with men. Just like he fucked us with no problem he'd do the same thing to you if you somehow convinced him to leave Bambi. Don't be so enamored with cumming. I taught you how to do it yourself."

"I'm sorry, mother. I was foolish and I'm so glad you smacked me so that I could see the error of my ways."

"Sorry is not a trait that suits us either. Just remain smart, Treasure. Am I clear?"

"I will never forget again," She said. "I promise, mother."

When there was a knock at the door Believe lowered down to her and whispered, "That's probably him. He enjoyed himself so much the other night that he wants more." She grinned. "We must be prepared to satisfy all of his needs until my plan kicks into the next level."

"Yes, mother."

"Now go see if it's him."

Believe stroked her long hair once more before Treasure opened the door. It was Mr. Kennedy himself. "Can I come inside?" Kevin asked with his hands tucked in his back pockets. "It shouldn't take long."

"Sure," Treasure smiled before backing up. "Come inside. Please."

Kevin walked deeper into the room and closed the door behind himself. "How are the accommodations?" he asked as if he didn't lick both of their pussies a day ago. "Are you both comfortable?"

Believe walked over to him and stood in front of his tall frame. "Kevin, we are adults here so there's no need to be creative in your reasoning for visiting. Now tell me what you really want." She stroked his dick once. "Whatever it is, we can take care of – "

He pushed her hand away and frowned. "I came by to say we can't get down like that no more. I was wrong and I'm taking the blame. I had some shit going on and I let the moment get away from me. But it won't happen again."

Believe glared at him because she hadn't expected his response. She and Treasure did world-class work on his body and she figured he'd be begging for more not cutting her off. What bothered her more was that Treasure stood next to her witnessing her failure.

"What won't happen again, Mr. Kennedy?" Believe said softly. "The fact that you had your dick in my mouth or my child's? What exactly are you referring to?"

Kevin shuffled. "Listen, I know it was fucked up but – "

"No, let me tell you what we're going to do...you're going to continue to satisfy me and in return we are going to continue to satisfy you. This will go on as long as I see fit. In other words, when I say stop. Not you."

His nostrils flared. "You not listening." He clenched his fists. "What we did the other night ain't happening no more." He pointed at the door. "It was a mistake and I don't repeat mistakes. Now you're welcome to stay here but – "

"How long have you been married?" Believe asked smoothly. "I mean I've seen you with your wife. You two have a bond and so it must have been for a long time. I see how you handle her in her drunkenness."

Kevin moved so close she could not walk around him if she tried. "I'd advise you not to threaten me with my wife again, bitch. Don't let my hospitality confuse you."

"Threaten you?" Believe giggled. "Who's threatening you? I'm just asking a question."

"How long I been married to my wife ain't none of your business. Now like I said, what happened between us will never go down again. You can stay here for a few more days but whether Abd is dealt with or not I want you out at that time." He turned to walk away.

"I'm not done with you, Kevin Kennedy. Don't turn your back on me because I'm not your precious wife. Besides, there's something more you must see. I'm sure you'll find it very interesting."

Kevin stopped walking. "What you talking about?"

"See, I forgot to tell you that I'm a freak. It's not enough for me to relive the best moments in my mind. I have to see them on repeat visually. That way I can preserve it for a lifetime."

"Are you gonna stop fucking around and tell me what's up?"

"I taped you." She giggled. "Correction, I taped the three of us."

Kevin rushed up to her and wrapped his hands around her throat. He squeezed so hard he saw her eyes redden. He resigned to killing her and explaining to Sarge later when Treasure hit him in the head with a glass. In slight pain he released Believe allowing her to catch some quick breaths before smacking Treasure to the floor.

When Believe dropped to catch some air he dropped down to confront her. "Where is it?"

"Where is what?"

"The TAPE BITCH! STOP FUCKING AROUND WITH ME!" He rose to his feet.

"That tape is some place safe. Don't worry; I'm not interested in anybody seeing it for now. But I will tell you what I want. To keep your secret."

"What the fuck is that?" he clenched his fists.

"A few million dollars placed in an overseas account that I use for emergency purposes only. I'm sure you can handle that because you're worth way more. We both know it."

"This not about no money, bitch," Kevin said. "I know it's not. Sarge is well off by fucking with us. So what you really want from me?"

She laughed. "You're right. It's not only about money but it's a start. The rest of my reasons are private. Now like I said, I will give you the overseas account information. After that, we'll talk about what else I need from you at that time. Not before."

CHAPTER TWENTY-ONE
RACE

My New Friend had been hitting me up nonstop but I wasn't interested anymore. Too much was going on in my life for experimental relationships. Drake's motto, No New Friends silently played in my mind.

Besides, something I couldn't explain was brewing between me and Bradley and he required all of my attention. Two days had gone by and we were having such a good time together it was effortless. Everybody seemed to be doing their own thing in the house so no one noticed that we were getting closer.

Bradley liked the same things I did.

He laughed at my jokes and me at his.

When I worked on my movie prosthetics he was in the basement helping me stir up the silicone to form my creations. When I talked about my dream of making it to Hollywood before the dope game he inspired me to not give up and that it was still a possibility.

He was a friend who shared my interests who also cared about me. Getting along with him was so easy I figured it was only right to tell him the truth.

We were eating turkey sandwiches I made when I said, "I need to be honest with you about something, Bradley. Something that makes me feel like a hypocrite."

He placed his sandwich on his red plate and gave me his undivided attention. "I'm listening."

I leaned against the refrigerator causing the apple magnet on it to fall to the floor. "I found out that Scarlett and Ramirez are having sex. It was some weeks ago although I don't know how long it's been going on."

Bradley laughed. "Come on, Race." He picked his sandwich back up and took a larger bite. "You can't be serious. The nigga may have shit with him but he not that crazy. You know that." He chewed and sat back confidently.

I rolled my eyes. "I wouldn't make something like this up."

He placed his sandwich down and wiped his hands on the paper towel on the table. "How did you find out? And when?"

"I saw them together, Bradley. I came upstairs to talk to her about something and I heard them saying they fucked before."

He ran his hand down his face. "This nigga got the nerve to be coming at me about you and he fucking Scarlett?" He pointed at the table.

I nodded my head. "Yes."

"Lately he been bringing up Roman stories of how when a brother dies his wife goes rightfully to the brother. Like a piece of property." He laughed softly. "Now I understand why."

I felt like killing Ramirez all over again for thinking he had the right to be with Scarlett just because Camp died. I realized at that moment that he was narcissistic. "This dude..."

"This shit is crazy." He paused. "So all this time you were using me to get at my brother? Like a pawn."

I moved closer. "It's not like how it sounds."

"Then explain it to me."

"At first I was flirting with you, only when I thought he would see us. But when you and I grew closer I realized you were more to me than just bait, but a friend. You still are now."

"A friend who you fucking."

"Bradley, I didn't know any of this would go down between us. Don't forget I tried to walk away."

"But you didn't make it far because you sat on my dick instead."

My lips pinched together. "I just wanted him to feel what I felt, Bradley. I wanted him to worry that he could lose me like I was losing him. After awhile I realized I never really cared in the first place. I mean, maybe it's really over between us. I don't know what to feel because everything's so raw."

"Listen, I know my brother. I might not have seen him fucking Scarlett but I know he would never leave you for her."

"And that's supposed to make me feel better? Your brother ain't no prize whether you realize it or not."

"No…I'm not saying that."

"Then what you saying?"

He took a deep breath. "I'm saying that he loves you and he might be smashing Scarlett but that's about it. There's no emotional situation between them. I wouldn't be surprised if he didn't tell her that to her face."

"It doesn't matter. He violated."

"And so did you, Race." He looked down at the table. "I mean…so did we."

I paced the floor next to him before stopping and flopping in the chair. "This shit is confusing. I mean...yes we did what we did...I'm talking about me and you...but he was fucking Scarlett just because he could."

"A wrong is a wrong. And didn't ya'll niggas use to do threesomes with each other all the time?"

"I'm so sick of people throwing that in my face. There are rules to this shit. Does that give him the right to fuck my sister-in-law?"

"Stop saying gives him the right. You know that's not what I mean. But ya'll invited the scenario into your bedroom so why get mad now that it's still going down?"

"First off I'm not fucking Scarlett. And you wouldn't understand." I shook my head. "I wasted my breath on you. I'm just now remembering that you're his brother."

He looked away from me. "Is it possible...and I'm not taking sides. But is it possible that what happened between me and you happened between them? Maybe they shared some secrets when they were in need and it got sexual? Because after we fucked we have no room to call that man on what he did, Race."

I sighed. "I don't know what's possible because that's not the point. All I know is that I gave Ramirez another chance and he fucked up again." I paused. "But there's something else. Something I have to get off my chest."

"What is it?"

"I been fielding calls from the Dope Phone. Basically I scheduled a fake meeting where two rival drug bosses will meet at the same time for a package. When they finally go to the location, instead of us being there a war will ensue and Scarlett will be to blame. I only did it with niggas we don't fuck with though so it shouldn't be major. Kevin was tired of both of them sets anyway."

His face screwed up and he leapt to his feet before moving toward me. "Fuck you talking about you fielded calls?" He yelled. "You messing with our money now?"

I got up and took a step back. "So the evil dope boy has revealed himself."

"I'm a dope boy before anything else, including being a brother or husband." He paused. "And I'm telling you to stop what you doing, Race. Or I gotta let Kev and 'em know."

I looked away. He showed me which side he was really on. "You're right."

"I'm serious!"

Now I wished I never told him. Suddenly I felt stupid and wondered if it was all worth it. "I said I would stop so leave it alone, Bradley."

He shook his head. "So you still wanna get the nigga jealous huh?"

I shrugged, still in my feelings about how he carried me. "It don't matter now."

"Too bad because suddenly I'm up for some games."

My eyes widened. "You serious?"

"Of course I am. All you had to do was ask in the first place. No need in giving me pussy and shit. Making a nigga think you were really feeling him because you sexy and everything. But I'll take it."

I hit his arm.

My phone vibrated and when I pulled out my cell I saw several missed calls and text messages from my New Friend. I didn't read the earlier messages but decided to review the last one he sent.

Text Message

New Friend: You gonna wish you didn't play
games with me bitch.

I laughed, dropped my phone back into my pocket
and sat in front of Bradley to discuss our plan.

The next afternoon Bradley and I were sitting in the
dining room playing cards after having lunch.
Knowing Ramirez would be up any minute to get
something to eat since he was a late sleeper, we were
sure we'd fuck up his head again when he saw us
together.

The moment we heard his footsteps, evident by the
way he slid across the hardwood floor with his black
and gold Versace slippers, we laughed loudly to fake
having an extraordinary time.

"I know you're cheating, Race," Bradley said
playfully as he looked at the cards in his hands. We
weren't even playing for real. The true game was
fucking with my husband's mind. "I don't know for
sure but I'm gonna find out after I put you over my
knee and spank that ass."

"You mean after I spank your ass," I said hitting his arm, holding it a bit longer than necessary. "Don't get mad because you losing, I just know how to play my cards." I winked at him. "Very well."

"Oh yeah, well I'm gonna find out how *good* you really are."

I guess he couldn't take it anymore because Ramirez stomped up to us and pushed the cards off the table. They fluttered around like falling birds before slapping onto the floor. "I thought I told ya'll I didn't want to see you hanging together no more?" He yelled, fists clenched at his sides and nostrils flaring like a bull. He wanted to box the both of us. I could see it. "Fuck is the problem?"

Bradley laughed in his face. "Man, I'm not 'bout to ignore my little sister because you don't want us to hang together. Now you coming down here fucking up the game too? Just relax."

"What about if I broke your jaw?" Ramirez asked through clenched teeth. "You think you could find it within yourself to stop then? With a little help."

"You getting way too serious now," I said to him seriously. I didn't want Bradley hurt.

"Shut the fuck up, Race." He pointed at me. "It's your fault anyway. Tempting my brother and shit. You know he can't handle that with Denim upstairs acting like *Hands That Rock The Cradle*. Obsessing over a kid that's not even hers. You playing yourself like a whore."

"What you just say to her?" Bradley asked as he stood in his face. "What you just call Race?"

And then something I wasn't expecting occurred. Bradley stole Ramirez in the jaw and the two of them went at it on the floor. Fists were flying and necks were held as they continued to fight over what I think was me.

When it was over and Ramirez stomped away I just knew Bradley was done with the games. We were sitting in the movie room, our favorite spot, when I gave him his out. "I'm so sorry about this, Bradley," I said as I placed a blue icepack on his eye which was a little swollen. "We can stop if you want, with the games. I didn't want you to get hurt."

He frowned. "Fuck no. All he did was make me angrier."

I looked at him seriously. "Why you really doing this?"

He shrugged and placed the icepack on the floor. "I don't know." He looked into my eyes and crossed his arms over his chest. "Have you ever..." He looked away again.

"What is it, Bradley? No more secrets between us remember?"

"Have you ever wondered if you married the wrong brother?"

I exhaled because the question was deeper than I expected to go. "I...I never thought about it. Never had a reason too." I looked at him. "Until now."

He nodded. "I don't know why I'm doing this for you, Race. I mean, the getting back at my brother part. I try not to ask myself questions that I'll never get a good answer to. All I know is that if you need me I'm here. Let's leave it at that for now."

RAMIREZ

Scarlett walked up to Ramirez who was sitting in the chair in the only available guest room. His lip was swollen and his leg was jittery. To put it simply he was mad as fuck.

"What happened to your face?" She asked. "And I thought we were going to play around tonight. I was looking forward to it."

Suddenly she did nothing for him.

He frowned and rubbed his chin before dropping his hand into his lap. "I think you were right." He pointed at her. "About Race knowing that we fucking." He looked away. "The only thing I can't understand is how she found out."

Scarlett's eyes widened. "Did...did she say she knew?" Her stomach bubbled and she farted softly. Luckily for her pride he didn't hear or smell it. "Did she say she saw us, Ramirez?" She grew louder.

"No!" He rubbed his knuckles.

She sighed in relief. "Then what happened?"

He shook his head. "Lately she been spending a lot of time with Bradley. I mean, all of a sudden these niggas acting like good girlfriends? Why? They don't have shit in common."

She shrugged. "Well did you ask them why they're so friendly all of a sudden?"

"They trying to make me think I'm crazy. Talking about they just cool and shit."

"What if they are? Who cares? We do what we do why not let them too?"

"Bitch, it ain't the same. I don't want nobody fucking my wife!"

"Whatever happens please don't tell her about us. I don't have anything else but this family, Ramirez. I can't lose it."

He leapt up, yanked her red hair and pulled it backwards. "Is she fucking Bradley, Scarlett? You better tell me now or I'm gonna kill you. I know you know something! Ya'll are friends."

Her face reddened as she softly touched the hand that was pulling the hair from her scalp, trying to calm him down. "Ramirez, I haven't spoken to Race in a couple of days. I don't know anything...but...but you're hurting me. If I had any idea I would've told you already. Please let me go."

He believed her and released her hair. Pacing the floor he said, "I gotta figure some things out. I'll get up with you later." He stormed away.

Ramirez walked up to Bradley's bedroom door only to see Denim sitting on the bed holding Master. Immediately he noticed her eyes looked off as if she wasn't the same person. "Denim, can I talk to you about something?"

"Sure...uh...come inside." She placed Master face down but kept a hand on his back as if she were protecting him. "What's up?"

Ramirez walked in and sat on the opposite side of her, the baby between them. "How are things going with you and my brother?"

She shrugged and forced a fake smile. "Fine I guess." She focused back on the baby, with wild eyes that seemed to swirl around when she spoke. "Why, what did he tell you?"

"Nothing...I...I just wanted to know if your relationship was going okay. I mean, I know there was some difficulty when he first came home from jail but I didn't know if that was still the case now."

"Everything is fine," she grinned and looked at Master again. "Couldn't be more perfect if you ask me." When Ramirez went to touch his nephew Denim went ballistic. "Keep your fucking hands off him, nigga! You probably didn't even wash them! Why do you nasty mothafuckas keep touching him with dirty paws?"

Ramirez jumped up. "Aye, Denim, you okay? Because you acting crazy now."

Slowly she allowed the frown to melt from her face that she replaced with a smile. Looking at him as if she didn't lose her mind she said, "Yes...of course I'm okay. Why you say that, Ramirez?"

He shook his head and walked out the door. *No wonder my brother spending so much time with my wife. His bitch crazy.* He thought. *But he not about to have mine.*

CHAPTER TWENTY-TWO

KEVIN

*K*evin paced the foyer of the living room as he tried to calm down and settle his mood. He took deep breaths to relieve himself of the anger he felt from having Believe and Treasure in his home and nothing worked.

He still wanted to commit murder. Or better yet, double homicide.

He needed his brothers and their opinions.

So one by one he rounded them up and brought them to the movie room for a private conversation, without their wives. It didn't take him long after looking at their screwed up faces for him to notice that something was up. "What's been going on? Why ya'll in here looking fucked up in the head?" he asked.

Bradley gazed at Ramirez and then Kevin. "I know you have more to say than that, man. So stop fucking around and tell me what's up?"

"Yeah…get to the point," Ramirez said.

"I'm serious," Kevin continued. "We haven't been alone since Camp died and I wanted to check in on my brothers. What, something wrong with that? A man can't break bread with his blood?"

Bradley shrugged. "I'm gonna keep my comments on brothers connecting to myself."

Ramirez laughed.

"What's funny?" Kevin asked him.

"I find it humorous that he can keep shit to himself now because when he's around the house he seems to have all kinds of word play for my wife."

Kevin frowned. "Hold up, bruh, I know you not accusing your brother of some disruptive behavior like that. Bradley smart enough not to go there with his little sister."

Ramirez pulled his own ear and crossed his arms over his chest. "All I'm saying is whenever I look up he's in her face. You can draw whatever conclusions you want upon that fact."

It took Bradley everything in his power not to reveal what he found out from Race. He would've said fuck it and let Kevin know everything but he had grown a similar bond with Race that Ramirez had with Scarlett. Except his bond was out of respect for Race.

Not only would bringing up the drama be too heavy for the moment but he would also feel like a hypocrite. He was determined not to betray Race's trust and for some reason it wasn't worth it for him to lose the loyalty he was building with her just to disgrace his brother. "I told you time after time that it ain't like that between me and Race," he lied. "So stop accusing me. Stop accusing her."

"Yeah, well you better hope not, nigga," Ramirez continued showboating.

Kevin wiped his hand down his face. Things were worse than he thought and he hadn't bothered to get to the real reason for the meeting. "We lost our brother. Not even six months ago. The last thing we need is to be fighting with each other. We have to honor Camp by making sure his son is taken care of and he needs all of us to make it happen. So let's not do dumb shit in our darkest hour."

"I'm not about to be brothers with no nigga who fucking my wife," Ramirez said as he turned his body away from Bradley and crossed his arms over his chest like a child. As if he didn't smash the fuck out of Camp's bitch.

Bradley bit his tongue to hold back on what he knew so hard it bled. "You know what, anybody accusing somebody as hard as you accusing me must be guilty."

Ramirez shuffled a little in his seat before chuckling once. "So you saying I'm fucking Bambi now?" He laughed harder. "Or wait, I'm fucking Denim who smells like baby throw up all the time?"

"Nah, bruh, not Bambi or Denim." He looked at Ramirez long and hard.

Ramirez, leveled with guilt, leapt up. "You know what, I don't have time for this shit." He paused. "Hit me when you want to say something real, Kevin. I'm gonna be in my room."

Kevin took one step toward him before Ramirez walked out. "I'm in trouble, man. And I might need your help."

Ramirez stopped in his tracks, turned around and faced him. "What's wrong, Kev?"

Kevin sat down and looked at the floor. "I…I fucked Believe." Bradley and Ramirez looked at one another before moving closer to Kevin, each sitting on his right and left side. "And Treasure," Kevin continued.

The Kennedy men were getting all kinds of pussy in the compound and they were moving recklessly at that.

Bradley wiped his hand down his mouth. "Fuck you mean? And Treasure? Ain't she a kid or something?"

"What it sound like I mean? I fucked both of them, man," Kevin continued. "And she ain't no kid. She over eighteen."

"Where this go down?" Ramirez asked. "And when?"

"In the guest room," Kevin said. "And at the same time." Ramirez and Bradley laughed. "Fuck difference does it make anyway?"

"You mean you did this shit with Bambi in this house?" Bradley asked pointing at the floor. "Knowing full well she has the potential to snap and kill niggas?"

"It was a fucked up night. I was tired of her drinking and wanted to catch some rest in the guest room. Believe walked in talking about she wanted some sleep and that she was trying to get away from her daughter. The next thing I know I'm sliding in my dick and five seconds later Treasure joined her. I still can't believe it went down."

"Sounds like you winning to me, bruh," Ramirez said. "Both of them bitches bad. Although I gotta admit the mother daughter thing a little weird for my taste but to each – "

"Stop fucking around, nigga!" Kevin yelled in his face. "They blackmailing me now. Got video on a nigga and everything. If Bambi finds out not only will our marriage be over but we all can see her fucking with the business too."

"So what we gonna do?" Bradley asked.

"Give me some time." Kevin looked at both of them. "I'm just letting you know in case we have to tuck a body. Or two."

CHAPTER TWENTY-THREE

BRADLEY

B *radley was in the kitchen warming up meatloaf from last night's leftover dinner when Sarah walked inside rubbing her growling belly. He was supposed to be hanging out with Race later in the poolroom but wanted to grab a bite first.*

Unfortunately now he had company.

Wanting nothing more than to fuck with him, Sarah sat at the table grabbed the plate that was meant for him and said, "Damn, I didn't know we had more leftover food, I would've eaten it already. You making enough for me right? Don't be greedy and take the whole thing."

Bradley's jaw twitched the moment he heard her voice. "Leave me alone, Sarah."

She laughed boisterously. "I'm gonna come out and ask, why don't you like me?" She grinned. "I know I'm not as beautiful or as charming as my precious daughter but you seem to hate me so much you can't even look at me most of the time."

"You know, Sarah, I blame myself for how you come at me." He turned around and looked at her.

"What you mean?"

"See, when I married Denim you believed that gave you the right to be in this family. To sit amongst kings." He pointed at her. "You one of them niggas who think by watching somebody else in the gym working out you'll lose weight too. But that ain't the case, Sarah. You don't belong in this family now and you never will."

She frowned. "I'm in this house ain't I?" She giggled. "Eating your food. Sitting on your furniture and living it up. Seems like I'm doing all right for myself if you ask me. And I'm gonna eat the last piece of that meat too." She pointed at the stove. "And you know why? Because I'm stronger than you, Bradley. I control Denim and that means I control your marriage too."

"How far do you think my love for Denim will allow you to talk to me like you know me?" Spittle flew from his mouth. "How long do you think I'm gonna allow you to breathe and move so recklessly in my house? I've killed niggas for less. What you think's keeping you alive?" He took two quick steps toward her.

She'd gone too far and she knew it.

She blinked a few times to clear her blurred vision. "All I wanted was something to eat, Bradley. Was just having a little fun with you. No need in — "

Bradley moved closer. "I'm a dangerous man, Sarah. And you my enemy. Do you know what I do to my enemies?" He looked down at her with disdain. "I asked you a question you fat bitch!"

Her posture stiffened as she suffered through his insult. "Wait until I tell my daughter what you just said to me. You gonna really pay for it now."

"Haven't you noticed, Sarah? The only thing Denim cares about in the world right now is Master. And you know why? Because instead of dealing with our daughter's death she had to pick up behind you and Grainger's shit. Now she's crazy. But I'm gonna get some payback for her starting today."

She tried to laugh him off but he wasn't amused, his stare fixed on her throat. "And how you gonna do that, Bradley?"

"You know, I'm tired of your face in my house and I think it's time I did something about that. Tonight."

Sarah looked into his eyes as he approached even closer and suddenly she felt ill to the stomach. Sensing his rage, she could suddenly see her life flashing before her eyes. "I'm going to my room."

She went to move until he said, "You gonna stay right there. You wanted my attention and now you have it. In fact, my attention will be the last thing you'll ever have on this planet."

"Bradley, you're taking things to the next level," she tried to smile. "I'm not gonna bother you anymore. You can have the meat. Just stay out of my way and I'll stay out of yours. I'll go to my – "

He stole her in the mouth and the flesh of her jaw opened under his blow immediately. Wanting to survive, she tried to scream but he caught her quickly by stealing her in the face again. Sarah dropped to her knees where he bent down and hit her repeatedly in the center of the nose with a closed fist. When she was barely moving he stood up, opened the kitchen drawer, grabbed the largest steak knife and stabbed her multiple times in the chest.

It had been a long time since he felt so much relief as he looked down at his work. She not only paid for the crimes of coming to his home uninvited but she also paid for what happened to him in prison. In that moment because he hated her so much he felt vindicated.

And then reality set in.

As he looked down at his bloody hands, holding the bloody knife over his wife's mother's bloody body he realized he hadn't thought things through. After all, this wasn't premeditated. His day was going good before she stepped up to him.

How was he going to get her out of the compound with the world watching?

By **T. Styles**   213

He decided there was one person he could go to for help and he hoped he could count on her.

Race's jaw hung as she sat in the recliner in the movie room and looked up at him. "I can't...I can't believe what you're saying or what you are asking me." She whispered. "Where is her body? And why would you come to me with this shit?"

"In your studio in the basement."

"What? But why you put her there?!"

"Keep your voice down." He took a deep breath. "I put her down there because there's so much creepy shit down there with your prosthetics that I figured even if someone caught a sight of it they wouldn't believe it was real. But we have to move quickly."

She jumped up and paced the floor. "Bradley..." words missed her and she didn't know what to say. It wasn't that she didn't see this coming, as much as he despised Sarah, but at the same time the murder was so final. So spontaneous.

What about Denim? How would she feel when she couldn't find her mother?

Suddenly Race was grateful for Denim's preoccupation with Master because that meant she wouldn't be looking for Sarah.

"I need your help, Race. I gotta get rid of her the best way I can."

"And what way is that?"

"I'm going off the compound to dump her body but first I have to cut her up in smaller pieces."

She leaned backwards. "Bradley, you can't be serious."

"I am, serious. And that's what I need your help with. If both of us do it, the body will be hacked up quicker than me doing it alone. Now will you help me? If you do I will be indebted to you for the rest of your life. Race, please help me."

Bradley and Race spent five hours in the basement of the compound destroying Sarah's body. Bradley took the upper torso and Race the lower part for efficiency's sake. It was the most brutal thing either of them had done but what surprised them was how quickly they did it together. They mirrored one another's dark personalities and it wasn't until that moment that it had become a reality.

When they were done they took in the blood around them and realized this one brutal act bonded them together for life.

Stuffing her flesh into individual black plastic bags that were more manageable, Bradley said, "This looks like one of your mangled body prosthetics." He raised her foot. "Doesn't it?"

Race removed the yellow rubber gloves stained with blood off and tossed them on the floor. She stomped across the room and after removing his gloves he approached her. "It's not funny, Bradley." She leaned against the wall. "Denim is my friend and contrary to what you believe I love her. This is gonna hurt her feelings."

"I'm sorry. Too soon to make jokes?"

Silence.

He took a deep breath and dropped the foot in the bag. "I know you didn't want to be mixed in with this but I'm glad you did because I couldn't do this without you." She looked away from him. "Do you hear me? I couldn't do this without you, Race and you came through for me. There's not another I could've turned to, not even my brothers."

She shook her head, looked into his eyes and sighed. "I know."

He walked up to her. "You're beautiful, Race." He kissed her lips. "Thank you for this." He kissed her again. "Thank you." Their breaths grew heavier as he kissed her neck. "And you smell so good, Race. So sweet...let me...let me feel you."

"Bradley, we can't be..." He covered her mouth with his lips before lifting her up. Using the wall as support he removed his dick and eased into her. She wrapped her legs around him and he noticed how soft and warm her pussy was. As if she'd been waiting.

"Why you wet and ready, Race?" He moaned. "Huh...if this scares you so much why you so fucking wet?"

She bit her bottom lip as he pounded into her slowly at first. "I don't know, Bradley...I don't know. There's something about you."

They continued to make love, Sarah's body parts leaking behind them.

CHAPTER TWENTY-FOUR

BAMBI

Abd called again…reminding me that soon my time was up.

Since Mitch was dead I knew there was nothing to do but wait for the destruction he was going to bring our way while praying to God that it wouldn't be final. That he wouldn't take everything from me I loved.

As I lie in bed, my head was swirling because it was hard for me to admit the truth. Kevin was right.

I was a drunk.

Looking at the ceiling I realized my world was coming to an immediate end, not only because of the beef I had on the streets but also the inner turmoil I was experiencing too. I had begun to savor alcohol so much that Kevin had taken to sleeping in the guest room, giving me more time to drink alone.

I'm sure it wasn't his plan to but it was the case.

I was now an official alcoholic.

Needing to wash my thoughts away I rolled over in the bed, on the sweaty part, grabbed my vodka bottle and turned it upside down, with the spout in my mouth I was quickly disappointed. One drop fell on my tongue, not enough to make me feel better. Things were so bad now that I needed a full bottle just to get through the day and another for the night.

Slowly I pushed over and stood on my feet before wobbling toward the door. The house seemed quiet as usual and that was beginning to be odd. It was as if everyone stayed within their little groups leaving me alone.

Maybe I liked it that way.

But where was Sarah?

Or my friends, Race, Scarlett and Denim?

Deep inside I wanted to see their faces every now and again but the other part of me wanted to be alone. To keep my privacy and drink in peace.

Two more days and Abd's threat would come to fruition but I don't think anyone else noticed. Ten days was nearing and he wanted Mitch!

Who was in a watery grave.

What were we going to do?

I was almost to the living room when I saw Believe moving toward me. I hoped she would walk around me because something about her I didn't like but she didn't. With a smile on her face she stepped into my pathway.

"Hey, Believe..." I said dryly.

She looked down at the bottle. "Bambi, you don't look well. Is there anything I can do for you?" She grinned. "Make you some coffee or something to eat? You seem like you could use a lot of help to me."

I cleared my throat. "Actually I need to relax and take a Tylenol. I'll be fine in an hour."

She sniffed the air. "You sure that's all you need? Because it sounds and smells like you need to push back also. Drinking gives you wrinkles in case no one has told you. I see a few crawling across your forehead as we speak."

I squinted my eyes. "What you just say to me?"

"You smell like a distillery, Bambi. And you look like you're running your face in the ground."

My stare was fixed on her. "You disrespectful ass bitch." I stepped closer. "You move in my house as if you know me."

"Don't be so shocked. You and me both know you been in your room sucking down bottle after bottle." She pointed at me. "You shouldn't be so surprised when you hear the truth. Consider it a favor. One woman telling another she's falling off."

I felt my body heat up. "You really jumping out there aren't you? Don't let my love for Sarge confuse you. You better recognize who you talking to or things can get real bad for your health. And your daughter's."

"Wow, you threaten my child?" She giggled. "And I do recognize who I'm talking too. A drunk."

Sarge…if I didn't love you she would be dead. I thought to myself.

My eyes widened. I wanted her dead and she'd be gone already but for Sarge being connected to my business. "I want you out my house tonight!"

She laughed. "You and be both know you can't throw me on the streets." She crossed her arms over her chest. "Besides, what would Sarge say? Since I know how you love him so much."

"I don't give a fuck what Sarge would say!" I stepped closer. "Because I want you gone tonight."

"So you don't care that my life will be endangered? Mine and my daughter's?"

"You should've thought about that before you tried me."

"What if I don't want to leave?"

Suddenly I raised the bottle and brought it down on the side of her face. Now her beauty was no longer so ravishing as a gash entered the flesh of her cheek and spilled out thick globs of blood that rolled into her mouth. "YOU CRAZY ASS WHORE!"

Something told me she wanted me to do that. As if she was looking for a reason to play the victim for Sarge.

"The next thing you gonna feel is a bullet," I announced. "Now I said get the fuck out of my house." I paused and moved closer. "Trust me, you don't want to say anything else. In all of your life you've never met a killer like me."

Holding her face she said, "Give me an hour. I should be gone before then."

"Make it fifteen minutes. You don't control shit around here." I rolled my eyes and walked past her. I walked into Race and Ramirez's room where I found a half empty bottle of vodka. Normally I had my own stash but it was depleted so I had to borrow theirs. Needing a buzz more than ever I grabbed it and stumbled back toward my room, barely able to stand on my feet. Once inside I flopped on the bed and popped the cap.

"Who the fuck she think I am?" I gulped half of the liquid. "Coming at me like she run my house. She deserved everything she got."

My thoughts were fleeting when suddenly the phone rang and it was Sarge. I started to ignore it but he was looking for some info on Abd and I needed to

Pretty Kings 4: Race's Rage

be ready to receive his call, even if he was coming at me about her. I just hope his wife didn't get to him yet. "Sarge..."

"How are you holding up, Bambi? I'm still worrying about you over there."

I sighed. "I'm okay..."

Silence.

"Sarge, are you there?"

"You been drinking, haven't you?" he asked. "I can hear it in your voice."

I wiped my hand down my face and rolled my eyes. "Yes. I've had a few gulps."

"I'm not gonna judge you. I love you and I know just like you pulled yourself out of all the other obstacles you'll do the same for this too."

"Any word on Abd?"

"None yet. But I'm on it." He paused. "How is everything else? With Believe and Treasure?"

"Sarge, I gotta hit you back, the baby crying."

"Bam—"

I ended the call, tossed it on the bed and continued to drink as I remembered all of the things Sarge has done for me. No matter how thick things got on the streets he always had my back. And this is how I repay him? By slicing his wife's face with a bottle and then throwing her to the wolves?

Sure she had it coming, but I could have her murdered in a freak accident after all of this blew over instead of going at her in my house. That way nobody would know it was me.

Doing that move to that whore's face was dangerous. Sarge was tied all into our business that Mitch used to run. One word from him and we would be destroyed and crippled.

For now, I had to bring her back.

I made a mistake.

I put the bottle on the dresser, after it was empty of course and grabbed my car keys. An hour had passed and I knew she was gone because one of the guards told me when she left. Still, I had to find her. Against my better judgment I walked out the house and toward my car and immediately one of my soldiers approached, concern written all over his face as he stared at me. "Mrs. Kennedy, would you like us to take you somewhere?"

"I'm fine, Marlo." I tried to walk around him but he blocked me. "Please get out of my way."

"Ma'am, you seem like you aren't well and Kevin instructed me to remind everyone to stay inside. I couldn't stop Sarge's family a minute ago but I'm begging you to heed his warming."

I flipped my hair over my shoulder. "I'm a grown woman! Now if I want to get in my car and leave that's on me."

"I still don't think it's a good idea."

I moved closer. "Must I remind you who pays you?"

He looked at me for a second, shook his head and stepped out the way. "No, ma'am."

"I didn't think so," I responded.

Once in my Mercedes I rolled out of the driveway. From the rearview mirror I could see the soldier on the phone and figured he was talking to Kevin. It didn't matter though. I had to bring Sarge's family back even if I had to drag them by their sew-in's.

I was halfway down the street on my block when suddenly my eyes felt as if concrete had been poured onto my lids and I could no longer control my car. Within seconds it swerved to the side of the road and crashed.

CHAPTER TWENTY-FIVE

RACE

I was sitting on my bed attempting to text my New Friend but he wouldn't respond. I don't know why I felt obligated to hit him again, especially after he disrespected me the way he did.

But I texted anyway.

I think part of me felt bad since I let him believe there was hope for us in a relationship when there wasn't. Who was I to have another relationship when I was married and full of drama. The other reason was that he knew too much. In our brief affair I revealed too many things.

Still, I was getting to a point where I was tired of misleading games. You could say that my emotional plate was full.

I was about to take a warm bath and meet Bradley in the movie theater to talk about Sarah. He was able to get her body away from the compound and dump it in a secret location. He wouldn't tell me where and I didn't want to know.

Sadly neither of us felt bad about what we did to her corpse and the weirdest part is that Denim didn't seem to know she was missing. She must've gotten her fucked up also when she was here, to make her not search for the mother she just had to have in our home. The house was so big and she was so caught up with Master that her obsession made her clueless and uninterested in much else.

Nothing mattered but that little boy in her world.

I dropped my robe, turned the hot water off and was about to slide inside the tub when suddenly I heard loud screaming within the house. I picked up my pink velvet robe, slipped it on and rushed toward the scene.

The noise was coming from Scarlett's room.

"I can't believe either of you doing this shit!" Bambi yelled, as she leaned against the wall. What looked like dried blood rested on her forehead and she appeared worse than I'd ever seen her before.

When I turned my head to see what she was yelling at I saw Ramirez trying to hop into his blue jeans and Scarlett standing in the corner of the room with a lavender sheet wrapped around her naked body. Both of them were looking at me guiltily as Bambi laid into them.

The secret was out.

They had been caught.

Stupid mothafuckas.

Couldn't even have an affair right!

I still had a few steps for my plan that Bradley didn't know about.

"Fuck is wrong with ya'll?" Bambi continued to yell at them. "What are you both doing? I'm not understanding this shit."

"I'm sorry, baby," Ramirez said rushing up to me, ignoring Bambi's question. "Scarlett doesn't mean anything to me and it's not what you think."

"Please forgive me, Race," Scarlett said as she remained where she stood. When her right breasts popped out she pushed it back inside and wrapped the sheet tighter around her body. "It was a mistake."

I was numb.

No anger.

No sadness.

No emotions at all.

I knew they were fucking and what I discovered in this moment was that I didn't care.

"Race, talk to me," Ramirez said before grabbing my shoulders and attempting to shake life back into me. Since he was using the same fingers that caressed Scarlett's body, suddenly I was jolted with anger as I shoved his hand off my arm. He didn't have the right to touch me. "I don't care what you do or who you do it with but don't touch me again. Ever."

Slowly he drew back his hand. "I want you out tonight, Scarlett," Bambi said while pointing at her. "Get your shit and bounce."

"She isn't going anywhere," Kevin said entering the room with authority. His jaw twitched as he came to the rescue of his brother. I'm not surprised he took his side but it was obvious he was angry at what he was seeing. It was in the way he was glaring at Ramirez. "She's family."

"So you think it's cool that she fucking Race's husband in this house?" Bambi continued pointing at her.

"No, I don't think it's right that she's fucking *my brother*. But she's still family and with the things we have going on out there we're not about to throw a family member on the streets."

"Are you sleeping with her too, Kevin?" Bambi asked.

"Bambi, please don't say that," Scarlett cried. "It was a mistake but I would never do that to you."

I frowned. "Oh, but you can do it to me though?" I asked.

The moment I said those words I felt dumb. There was that hypocritical shit again. I had been with Bradley multiple times and yet I pointed the finger at the white homie who fucked my husband. Still, as far as I was concerned they started it all. But for their relationship I would've never gone there with Bradley. Basically our affair was their fault too when you thought about it.

"You know what, I don't care what she does. Let her stay, let her leave, just as long as she stays the fuck away from me."

"Baby, you have to believe me when I say it didn't mean anything," Ramirez continued to beg as he walked around me in our bedroom like he was a vulture waiting to eat my rotting flesh.

Any other time I would be all ears but now I was indifferent, didn't care if he said a word to me or not.

Because what I know is this, Ramirez hated me for growing up. For not being the little girl he met holding the silicone over a nigga's car, dropping it by accident, so that he could kill him and save my life. So he could save the day.

The drug life had made me stronger and I was no longer a bitch in distress. His specialty was soft females who needed his assistance and I did not.

Now that I think about it I'm pretty sure he loved the drama. That's why he wanted a weaker bitch, me in my younger day. His performance wouldn't go over on a harder female so queue in Scarlett who just lost her husband and had nothing left.

"I guess I wanted someone to hold, Race and I went to her. But I don't care about her. She means nothing! At all!"

"It never means anything to you, Ramirez," I sighed. "That's the problem. It didn't mean anything when you were fucking Carey and fell in love and it didn't mean anything with Scarlett. Maybe if you started giving a fuck you wouldn't be caught up in so much shit."

"You know that's not what I meant!" He yelled.

"But you know what, now things make so much sense." I pointed at him and winked.

"What you talking about?"

"The way you kept accusing Bradley of being with me. The guilty always tell on themselves when the truth hits them in the face." I paused. "It's officially over, Ramirez. You can consider yourself a free agent."

KEVIN

Ramirez walked into the movie room coolly, trying to act as if his world had not been rocked. Kevin was waiting and told him to meet him within the hour. The moment he entered the space Kevin stole him in the jaw, shaking his facial plate and knocking him to the floor. Ramirez attempted to defend himself by throwing a blow but Kevin blocked it and hit him again.

"Fuck you do that for?" Ramirez said rising to his feet, before flopping in one of the recliners.

"You took advantage of that girl and you had no right to do that shit, man." He pointed at him. "Nigga, are you crazy? Them girls tied into our money! It ain't about just busting a nut, it's about our lifestyle! Here I am worried about Abd and the real threat going down in my own house!"

Ramirez stroked his throbbing jaw. "As much pussy as you get around here and you coming at me about my slide?"

Kevin moved closer. "Let me be clear, I would have never, ever, fucked one of my sister-in-laws. EVER! Not because I don't find each one of them attractive, because I wouldn't want them getting all emotional around my money." He pointed at the floor. "You could've had your pick of any woman in the world. Why would you fuck with one of them? How you think Camp would feel about you smashing his wife?"

For the first time since shit went down Ramirez felt guilty. Slightly anyway. "It just happened man. I got bored in here and – "

"Haven't you learned anything from Cameron, Thick and the rest of them niggas at Emerald City who lost their operation fucking with their bitches? Did their downfall tell you anything? There is nothing more dangerous than a woman scorned. You don't shit where your money rests, man."

"I said I'm sorry."

"I want you to stay away from that girl." He pointed a long finger in his face. "You were wrong and if shit gets out of hand behind this you gonna pay."

By **T. Styles**   233

Kevin was about to walk out when Ramirez said, "So you don't think this is similar to you hitting Believe and them off with some dick in this house?"

"Not even close, nigga. I would put a bullet in each of them bitches heads before I ever let them fuck with my money. I can't do that with Scarlett and them." He took a deep breath and wiped his hands down his face. "She's family...and you better hope your actions didn't fuck with our money. It was a bad move, one that's gonna come back and haunt you." Kevin stormed out.

CHAPTER TWENTY-SIX

BAMBI

Standing in the living room, I took a swig as I stood in front of Race and Denim who had Master in her arms. They were sitting on the sofa looking up at me like I was the crazy one. But from what I saw I wasn't the only person who lost her senses. Lately Denim's eyes seemed wild as she looked at Scarlett's boy, almost as if she was obsessed with his presence.

But who was I to point fingers?

My mind was flying as I tried to understand what I saw with Scarlett and Ramirez in the attic. I walked into the room to ask her to let me use her truck since my car was crashed down the street but her door was locked. Using the key we had when Mitch was upstairs I let myself inside only to find Ramirez fucking her from behind on the floor.

"Why does it feel like I'm more angrier than you are, Race?"

"Maybe because you're drunk." I stepped toward her ready to hit her in the jaw and she stood up. "I'm sorry about that, Bambi. But you can't tell me how to feel. It was my husband who cheated not yours. Let me deal with it my way." When her phone beeped she took it out and sat down.

Lately, whenever I saw her anyway, she seemed more preoccupied with her cell and I wondered if she had someone else in her life. Maybe that was the reason she didn't seem shocked that her man was fucking our friend. "Couldn't be my husband."

"Let it go, Bambi. I think niggas do what niggas gonna do." Race shrugged. "Let 'em all fly if you ask me."

My eyes widened. "Niggas gonna do what niggas do? Fuck is wrong with you?"

She slammed her phone down. "LET ME HANDLE MY MARRIAGE! WHILE YOU FOCUS ON YOURS!"

"Damn, Race, you gonna scare my baby being so loud and ghetto!" Denim yelled. "Calm down with all that noise."

We both looked at her. "Hold up...you do realize that isn't your baby," Race said to her. "He's your nephew-in-law at best."

Denim gazed at us and then back at Master. "You know what I mean." She kissed his forehead. "He's all mine."

Race sighed and focused on me. "I want you to let this go, Bambi. This ain't your war to fight. Besides, what the fuck happened to your face and your car?"

"I told you already," I said. "I swerved to hit a deer and crashed into the signpost up the block," I lied. "One of the soldiers came and got me and brought me back. That liquor I got off your dresser seemed extra potent. Now why do you seem so easy going about Scarlett?"

Race's eyes widened before she looked away from me and pleaded. "Please, let this—"

"Something's happening," Kevin said entering the living room. Ramirez and Bradley followed quickly behind him.

"What's wrong?" I questioned.

"You know what...." He walked up to me, took the bottle of liquor from my hand and flung it across the room. It crashed against the wall and shattered into a million pieces. I was so angry I was trembling. That was my last bottle and now I was gonna have to sneak outside to get some more. And since we are being hunted that was easier said than done.

"Why you do that?" I yelled at him.

"First off where is Sarah and Sarge's people?" Kevin asked as he scanned the room.

I backed away, flopped on the chair and sighed. "I don't know where Sarah is but I put Sarge's family out earlier today." I took a deep breath. "Now what's wrong? Why you come in here like you on fire? Throwing my shit on the wall."

Kevin looked back at his brothers. "Something is going on with our customers. I just got a call that a gun battle broke out somewhere down Baltimore by two rival gangs. The thing is people saying we set it up."

"Why?" I asked.

"Because we told them we were delivering work to the warehouse where it went down. But we never serve two rivals at the same time. It's dumb."

"I know, Kevin! So why you coming at me like this is my fault? I'm not that irresponsible to give an order like that. The last instruction I gave was that everyone was to be cut off until this Abd shit blew over."

"If it wasn't you then who was it?" Kevin continued.

"You know Scarlett fields the calls."

He looked at Bradley. "Go get her for me, man."

Denim stood up. "I'm gonna put the baby in my room and see if I can find my mother to watch him. I'll be right back."

I rubbed my throbbing temples because the pressure was mounting. What was happening to my family? And now my business?

A few seconds later Bradley came back with Scarlett who was wearing a grey sweat suit that seemed to drown her curves. Her hair was pulled in a loose red bun that sat on top of her head and she looked smaller, almost child-like for some reason.

Suddenly I felt sorry for her.

Maybe out of guilt, Ramirez couldn't even look her way.

It's no secret. I loved Scarlett. Like a sister, which is why her betrayal hurt me the most. I would've never saw her doing something like this to anyone of us but it didn't stop the love I had for her in my heart.

Still, Ramirez was just as responsible and I hated that no one seemed to care.

"Yes," Scarlett said in a soft voice, leaning on the wall.

"Scarlett, a war is happening and we got word that you fielded calls saying we were delivering work tonight." Kevin said. "With two rival drug gangs at the same time? Did you do that?"

She rubbed her temples and I realized she didn't remember. "I...I don't know why I would have done that. The phone hasn't even been ringing enough lately for me to make such a statement. I thought that was weird, but figured since we weren't making drops right now that could've been the reason. I mean, are they saying that it was me?"

"Let me see..." Kevin made a quick call and we all waited for the verdict. "Louie, who did Chris say led his people to the warehouse? From our end?" He nodded his head. "Thanks, man, I'll hit you back in a second." He dropped the phone back into his pocket. "They saying your name."

Her eyes widened. "But…that's not like me. I knew the rules." She scratched her head. "I wouldn't have—"

"Do you realize the bloodshed tonight in our name? Fourteen niggas died fighting and it's our fault. We looked like we were setting mothafuckas up and for what?"

"Kevin, I'm so sorry," Scarlett cried. "Lately my mind has been messed up. Maybe it happened that night Master was in the tub. I'm so—"

"You gotta go, Scarlett," Kevin said. "This mistake is too big and I don't want you in here while we sorting things out. I can't trust you anymore."

Her jaw hung. "Kevin, please. This the only family I've ever known. I can't go back to—"

"Get the fuck out my crib!" He yelled pointing at the door. "And my nephew stays here."

Scarlett looked at me, then everyone else. I didn't know what she was thinking but I could tell she felt gut punched by his words. Suddenly I wanted to defend her even though I was trying to put her out a minute ago myself. But why was it easy for him to throw her out when money was involved but not when she was caught fucking Ramirez?

Typical NIGGA-BROTHER shit.

Sometimes I can't stand these niggas.

"I'm sorry, for everything I did." She cried, wiping her tears with her fists. "And Race I know you will never forgive me but I love you and will spend the rest of my life thinking about how I wronged you."

"Yeah, aight..." Race said rolling her eyes.

Slowly Scarlett moved toward the door and into hell.

When she left Kevin's phone rang again and he answered. He was silent for a minute before saying, "Don't say that shit, man!" He said to the caller. "FUCK!"

I stood up and walked over to him. "What, Kevin?"

He dropped the phone into his pocket. "Sarge has been killed. By Abd's people. I'm sorry, Bambi."

I dropped to my knees.

I felt too much loss. Sarge was like a father to me even though mine was still alive. They hit our crew hard with that move and we were on the losing end of this war.

Roman stepped into the Kennedy compound with her trusted friend Owen. The hoody she wore covered most of her pretty face with the exception of her green eyes. Bambi, Race, Denim, Kevin, Bradley and Ramirez were standing at the door waiting on her. She was our best killer and when she was on the job we knew something would go down to our advantage.

"What you find out?" I asked, hands stuffed in my fatigue pants.

"There's a wedding going down this weekend. It looks like everyone will be there, including Abd and his son." She paused. "I can try to get inside but it may be impossible."

"It's obvious you have some plan. What is it?" Kevin continued. "Because I know for a fact security will be steep. Especially after what they took from us. In my opinion he knows we will be out hunting."

"I got my ways and I'll leave it at that," Roman said.

"If it works, we will be indebted to you," Kevin advised. "We need this dude out of our lives, Roman. He's causing major destruction."

"Like I said I don't know if it will go through. Abd and his men will be there but I can't think of a better time to stop him then now. All we have to do is execute procedure and I'll need help from you all too."

"Then we better get started going over the details," I said. "Like yesterday."

RAMIREZ

They walked into the dining room and hatched over the layout on how to bring Abd to his knees. Hours passed and suddenly Ramirez's phone rang. He looked at his family and down at his cell. "I'm gonna take a piss. Be right back."

"Nigga, don't make no announcements. Just hurry the fuck back. We have a lot to go over tonight," Kevin said.

Race looked at him and smiled sarcastically as he moved toward the bathroom. She drew her own conclusions about who was on the phone but she kept them to herself.

Once inside the bathroom he took a deep breath and answered. "What's up, Scarlett?" He leaned against the wall and looked at his reflection in the mirror. "Because I'm busy right now. Too much going on in these streets."

"I need your help, Ramirez. Kevin cutting me off but I don't have any money to get a place to stay. I don't have anything."

Ramirez looked around the bathroom. "Listen, I'm gonna need you not to hit my phone no more."

"But, Ramirez — "

"We got caught, Scarlett! Now I gotta clean this shit up and make good with my wife. The pussy was decent, no doubt. But not decent enough to throw away what I have with her. You knew this would happen. Remember or motto? Fuck now and deal with the consequences later? Well here are the consequences."

"Ramirez, please, I just need a few bucks until — "

"Leave me the fuck alone!" he ended the call that left her stranded.

CHAPTER TWENTY-SEVEN

RACE

I was sitting in the movie room thinking about the plans for tomorrow. I wasn't sure if what we went over would work because fucking with Abd and his crew was suicidal but we had to make a move. We'd never went against a rival like this before, not even the Russians were as vicious or had as many people working for them that Abd did.

Still, for some reason I was starting to realize the threat within our family was greater than anything Abd could do to us. We were killing ourselves from the inside. And the way we hated each other now we were doing a good job for him.

Scarlett was thrown out like a sack of trash. I was fucking Bradley. Denim was baby crazy. Bambi was drunk and Kevin was doing only God knew what. You could never tell with him but I'm sure the nigga had secrets.

I grabbed the glass of wine sitting next to me and was about to take a sip when Denim walked inside. "Hey, I been looking for you." She scratched her face. "Do you know what happened to my mother?"

I moved uneasily in the chair. "No…where she go?"'

"She's not here, Race. I looked all over this house and I couldn't find her anywhere. Why? You think she mad at me or something?"

I stood up because her standing over top of me made me nervous. Denim had a way of faking dumb only to snap moments later while revealing she already knew the truth. "I'll be more than happy to help look for her but if you searched the compound and couldn't find her maybe she left. I mean, she was beefing with the family and things probably got uncomfortable here."

Denim looked into my eyes as if she was trying to read my mind, forcing me to send my eyes downward. How did she know to come to me? Had Bradley sold me out? I didn't think that was possible because he had done the legwork on that murder. I was only on cleanup but I was unsure.

"Something ain't right," she said putting her fingers over her heart. "I feel it in here."

Aw shit.…

My heart thumped in my chest and I moved around uneasily. This was it, I was gonna have to wreck my friend or else she would get the best of me.

Suddenly Denim flopped on the chair and threw her face in her hands. Sobbing uncontrollably she said, "She left because I didn't want her to stay. She kept begging to spend some time with me and I didn't want to be bothered, Race. I didn't want to be with her. She was an itch on my life and she wouldn't go away."

Relief overtook my body because at least she wasn't blaming me. But I didn't want her sitting with the pain of her mother's disappearance either. "How you figure it's your fault, Denim? You gave her a place to stay. Even going against the family to make it happen because that's how much you love her."

"But she knew I didn't want her here. She knew everybody else felt the same way too so she bounced."

I sat next to her and rubbed her back. "Why do you continue to take responsibility for the actions of grown people? If she did leave she wanted to go and that's her choice. Don't beat yourself up about it."

"It's not just her, it's everything. Bradley not fucking me the way he used to. It's like he's holding something back from me. Why doesn't he trust me because I know something happened in prison? Our marriage hasn't been the same since he came home. All I want is for him to talk to me, to say something."

I removed my hand off her back and placed them in my lap. Looking at my nails I said, "Well maybe you should let me help with the baby more. To give you some free time."

She frowned at me. "You? What you know about babies?"

"That's hurtful, Denim. Just cause I can't have one don't mean I don't know nothing about them."

"That's not what I meant."

"Then make yourself clearer."

"You're not the mother type of person, you said it yourself a few days ago. In my room. You're more into the gore-horror-movie type shit and Bambi is more into the liquor bottle. With his mother gone who's better suited to take care of that boy than me?"

What bothered me the most was that she was telling the truth. Still, she was no more the kid's mother than Bambi or I and if she wanted her marriage something had to give.

"All I'm saying is that you have to sacrifice bonding with the baby if you want to re-build with Bradley. He loves you, Denim. But you gotta meet him halfway. Me and Bambi ain't the best mothers in the world but we still women and can help with our nephew."

"You're right...but I don't know how to let that baby go. When I look at Master it's like I'm looking into Jasmine's eyes again."

"But he's not Jasmine and those aren't her eyes."

She frowned. "You don't think I know that? You don't think I realize he isn't my little girl? It still don't make me love him less."

I sighed and decided to kick it raw. "Fuck all this crazy shit...at the end of the day it's the baby or Bradley. You gonna have to make a decision on what you want to do. Do you want him or not, Denim? It may seem like hard work but it's really that simple."

She looked at me and then out at the blank movie screen. Standing up she wiped her hands on her thighs and sighed. "I gotta go check on the baby. I'll talk to you later."

Wow.

Guess that was her answer.

I was still in the theater when Bradley walked inside and plopped next to me. "I saw her leave." He sighed. "So you're watching a blank screen now?" He asked.

I smiled. "Not really. I'm just envisioning how tomorrow gonna play out. With Abd." He looked at me but remained silent and I knew what he was waiting for. "Yes, I already know, Bradley. It was all my fault that them gang members died and I let Scarlett take the rap for it."

"You made a mistake out of anger. It happens."

I looked into his eyes. "I love you, Bradley. And I know I shouldn't love you but I do."

He swallowed. "Wow. Didn't see that coming."

"I'm sorry..."

"No...I love you too, Race."

I felt as if the breath had been removed from my body. "But...but we—"

"I know what you're about to say. And you're right. We can't point fingers at Ramirez and Scarlett and stay together." He paused. "It's over. We'll always have these moments and the ten days we were locked down. It will be our secret."

I nodded and a tear fell down my cheek. He kissed it away.

"I can't do to Denim what Scarlett did to me and live with it. I didn't expect to feel this way for you but its too late. You're the best and the worst thing that has happened to me at the same time. How is that possible?"

He smiled at me, kissed me on the lips and walked out.

I missed him already.

CHAPTER TWENTY-EIGHT

THE KENNEDY'S

The soft overhead light glistened against the elaborate table settings around the perimeter of the wedding hall. Just one silver fork alone was worth enough to pay a hood nigga's rent for a month. And yet it was just one of the many finishing touches in place for Abd Al-Qadir's descendent, who was marrying his new bride via an arranged marriage within an hour.

The ceremony had yet to take place but everyone who was anyone in Saudi Arabia was invited to the mystical celebration in a small suburb of Washington D.C.

All were happy.

Arabic music played quietly in the room and was intermixed with popular American tunes, as Jawad was a fan of the culture.

Finally it was time.

The door opened and Abd, Jawad and his groomsmen walked to the front of the hall and awaited the arrival of his bride. Mixing the Middle East with the West, the audience was in awe at the multi-million dollar ceremony unfolding before their eyes.

The celebration was moving art.

A spectacle to behold if that's what you were in to.

Jawad was handsome but Abd was striking. Standing over six feet tall, he possessed rugged good looks that appealed to women of all nationalities. The hairy beard that connected to the lower half of his face was coal black and resembled a mink coat.

Dressed in a white suit and a red and white Keffiyeh, Abd strolled over to his son and placed a firm hand on his shoulder. From a far he noticed that Jawad was jittery and feared he would walk away from his destiny, as he threatened to many times before. "Don't worry, she'll make you happy, Jawad," Abd said as he looked down at his son, before smiling in a fake manner at the crowd. He was doing his best to calm the suspicions of the guests whom he was certain noticed his son's anxious mood.

The man looked as if he wanted to be anywhere but in that bitch, locking his life with someone he barely knew.

Jawad smiled although it only lasted for a moment. "I know, father. She's beautiful and—"

"Our family needs this marriage to go off without a hitch," Abd said harshly. "You know Rana's father is powerful in Saudi and here in America as well. With their support we can do many things, son. Do not destroy this for our family because you are unwilling to do your part and make her your wife." His voice grew deeper. "It will be a grave mistake."

He nodded. "I understand father," he whispered. "And I don't mean to sound ungrateful. Maybe it's the nervousness you detect and I will do my best to rid myself of this weak emotion at once."

Abd placed a firmer hand on his shoulder. "Good. You are my son and we are never fearful about a future we control. Don't worry; even as your wife you will have many women but also many heirs." He pointed at him. "The choice will always be yours unless it conflicts with mine."

Jawad shook his head. "Yes, father. And again, I will pull myself together."

Just then the music grew louder as everyone in the room rose to show respect to Jawad's veil covered wife. A small smile spread across Abd's face as he looked at her henna decorated hands holding an elaborate bouquet of colorful roses speckled with gold, red and white.

Standing in the wrong place, Abd walked away and reclaimed his position as Jawad's best man and waited as the others did for the ceremony. This wedding would net the once over billionaire more money than he could spend and he needed it to go through seamlessly.

But something was wrong.

Where was Rana's father who was supposed to walk her down the aisle?

Why was she coming to enter the next phase of her life alone?

His question was answered when suddenly the bride lifted her veil and Abd was gut punched when he realized he was staring into the eyes of Bambi Kennedy. It was a takeover of an amazing kind. Something he had not prepared for.

Speckled in several other positions Bambi's crew rose with powerful assault weapons aimed at Abd and his guests. "I am Bambi Kennedy," she announced, as she dropped the bouquet that was used for nothing more than a cover for her weapon. "And I am here to right the wrongs that have occurred to me." Her focused moved toward Abd who was throwing her looks that could kill. "Sadly enough, most of you will die tonight. So I suggest you say your prayers."

Suddenly within the crowd, Race, Kevin, Bradley, Ramirez, Roman and Owen all rose holding assault weapons aimed at Abd and his son. It was a takeover Abd didn't see coming.

They gained entry from an insider that Roman connected with, along with the proper credentials and outfits to make them blend in with the ceremony. Being African-American meant their dark skin and partially hidden faces, went unnoticed amongst the Middle Eastern attendees.

Now on their feet, they fired into the crowd killing men and women with their extreme gun power. The plan? Total destruction.

Bambi was about to shoot Abd when he yanked her and held her in a one-armed headlock. Every time she tried to move he would press against her throat with his bicep, tightening his grip on her oxygen.

"If you kill me I will break her neck! Do you hear me? I will crack her throat!" Abd yelled out

loud at Bambi's entourage. "You declare war on the day of my son's wedding so trust me I'm serious! Put the weapons down! NOW!"

"GET THE FUCK OFF MY WIFE, MAN!" Kevin yelled. In that moment with all of her errors he realized he needed her. If she died a part of him would go too.

"I said put the fucking weapon down!"

Abd squeezed Bambi's neck harder and Kevin could see her face reddening. "Okay, man, okay, you have it." He paused. "Just don't hurt her please."

"You come into this celebration for my son and you do this to me?" Abd yelled. "Do you know who I am? Do you know what I am capable of? PUT THE FUCKING WEAPONS DOWN! I'm in charge! Not you!"

"Father, let her go." Jawad begged. "Please."

"SON, STAY IN YOUR PLACE! This is between me and the Kennedy's." Abd continued, ignoring his son's pleas.

"Okay, okay, you have it." Kevin relented. He looked at his entourage. "Put the weapons down." He was willing to die for his woman because there was no life without her.

By **T. Styles** 257

Slowly everyone complied except Roman.

Kevin frowned as he looked over at her. "Fuck you doing? Put the gun down! You gonna get Bambi killed."

"Calm down, Kevin," Roman said softly. "Everything's cool here. I'm gonna put my hammer down right now." She slowly lowered her body until she was halfway bent but instead of releasing the weapon on the floor she rose and with sniper accuracy fired once, hitting Abd in the center of the head. Blood splattered on Bambi's face as Abd released the hold along with his last breath.

The big bad threat was gone.

Kevin and the others breathed a sigh of relief.

Seeing his father killed, suddenly Jawad turned around and focused on the murderous army. "I will not say anything if you let me go." With the largest peril being eliminated, the Kennedy Klan picked up their weapons and moved closer to Jawad. "My father and I were not close and I will walk away. I promise."

"I'm sorry," Roman said. "Your death was in the deal too." Without another word she shot him in the face.

Race, Bambi, Ramirez, Bradley, Kevin, Roman and Owen stood outside of the wedding hall with Rana, Jawad's fiancé. She was the secret to their success. Realizing she would rather die and live alone in America, she sacrificed the lives of her husband, his family and even her own to be free and help Roman.

Jawad's constant abuses and disrespect made her feel dead inside and she was willing to do anything for freedom.

It was Roman who watched from a far while doing her investigative work on Abd and his family. She saw how Jawad treated her with disdain when Abd was not watching. The woman looked miserable. Having been abused for some part of her life she knew first hand what it was like to be fed up and was positive that with the right words she could convince Rana to take sides with them and with a little effort she was correct.

So during a fitting for her wedding dress in Washington D.C., Roman approached and the rest was history. After details on who was coming and where they would be seated, she was able to help her partner in crime and win her freedom.

"You don't know how much this means to me," Rana said shaking Roman and then the Kennedy's hands. *"Finally I can live my life. Without being worried about if I will live or die any minute."*

"How will you survive?" Bambi asked. *"Everybody you know here is dead."*

She sighed. *"Yes, this is true, but it's better to be alone than to be in a relationship with a mad man. Marriage isn't what it's cracked up to be if you hate one another as much as I did Jawad."*

Bambi, Kevin, Race, Bradley and Ramirez all looked at one another. Considering the things that went on in their family recently they realized they had a lot of thinking to do.

"Well, I must go, to begin my new life. I wish you all luck and thank you again, Roman, for everything." Rana smiled, walked toward one of the many white Bentley's in the parking lot in front of the hall and rolled off.

Bambi turned to Roman. "Thank you so much, Roman. You saved our lives."

"Yes, and my debt is finally paid." Roman said firmly as Owen stood at her side.

Bambi frowned, confused at her statement. "What you talking about?"

"The contract we had together indicated I owed you a hundred lives. I've paid that sum two times over with the massacre that occurred inside this building." She pointed at the hall. "I'm no longer indebted to you or the other Kennedy's."

Bambi looked at her family and back at Roman. In the heat of the moment she forgot all about the agreement. "Is there nothing we can do to put you back on? We'll double your salary if that's what you want."

"Money is not an issue," Kevin said. "You know that, Roman."

"I know, but I think I'm gonna go at it alone. I appreciate the offer though. Don't worry about it. You'll be hearing from me sooner than later. That you can believe." She tapped Owen on the shoulder and they walked to a white van and pulled off.

"Why do I have a feeling she's gonna be more trouble for us than anything we could have imagined?" Bambi asked the group.

"I was thinking the same thing," Race said. "Although I don't know why she would be beefing with us. We ain't do shit to her."

"If she does make a move we're Kennedy's," Kevin replied. "We're ready for anything."

EPILOGUE

TWO MONTHS LATER

RACE

Race turned off the shower and stepped out just as Ramirez was coming inside the bathroom. "Bambi said breakfast is ready. You coming down?"

Race grabbed the towel and wrapped it around her damp body. "She still into the Everybody-Eating-Every-Morning-Together kick?"

He chuckled. "Yes...I'm kind of glad she's forcing us to eat together though. It's the only time we all spend some time alone. Since Abd has been taken care of we all so deep into the dope game again we hardly see each other."

"I'm still not sure about everything. She put the vodka bottles up but exchanged them for Mimosa's. She acts like we don't know she's drinking harder. I'm getting worried about her, Ramirez."

"And I'm getting worried about us. And our marriage."

She giggled at that nigga. "You so used to getting things when you want them that you don't allow anybody else a chance to go through their process. I'm not ready to connect with you, homie."

"I just don't want you to leave me. You got me sleeping in the guest room like some fag only to let me into our bed when you want to be fucked or have your pussy eaten."

"You don't have to eat it if you don't want. I can play with my clit and still get the same satisfaction."

"I will lick every part of your body, Race, you know that. But I'm a man and you trying to make me feel like I'm your—"

"Side chick? Hoe? The other woman?" she laughed. "All the things that you've done to me and to other chicks? How does it feel? Like it much?"

He wiped his hand down his face in frustration. "There's no getting through to you is there?"

"I'm doing stuff on my time and right now I'm not feeling like being your wife. You slept with my friend, Ramirez. If you don't like the way things going on sign the divorce papers I stuck to your door last night. Either way I don't give a fuck no more."

"I would've never hit Scarlett off if you would've responded to me. If you would've let me know you cared."

"I WANTED YOU TO FIGHT FOR ME! I WANTED YOU TO FIGHT FOR OUR MARRIAGE! Not sleep with someone just because you could. You have a way of making me feel disposable and I'm tired of the drama, Ramirez. Tired of the games and tired of the emotional tug and pull loving you brings. So you can do whatever you want but you won't bully me into forgetting that you fell in love with Carey or fucked Scarlett. That is where it all started. You may have forgotten but I didn't. I will never let you hurt me again. That is one thing I'm certain of."

Race slipped into her red sweat suit.

"Wow, you really are gonna drag this out huh? You really plan to make me feel guilty for the rest of my life?"

She giggled and he was about to walk out until she said, "Aye, Ramirez, I forgot to show you something right quick."

Things may have quieted down but she was still on her revenge shit. She knew there was one thing he would hate more than anything and it was time to reveal her secret.

He walked up to her. "What is it?"

She removed her cell phone from her pocket, skipped to a video and hit play. He snatched it from her and his eyes widened when he saw Race sucking Bradley's dick as he begged her not to stop. Bradley had two hands on Race's head and everything. The video had been taken when Bradley was inebriated and they were in the movie room. He had no idea she had filmed them. Ramirez continued to watch the video until Bradley came into her mouth and she swallowed.

The phone dropped out of his hand and he stole her in the stomach. "You dirty bitch!"

She giggled and doubled over in pain. "I knew about you two way before Bambi caught you. So my question is, handsome, how does it feel?"

He scratched his head as a tear ran down his cheek. He was certain that she'd never been with another man before him and to find out the man after him was his brother cracked his world. "Why would you do this to me?"

"Because you deserved it." She rubbed her stomach that was throbbing.

"I'm about to step to this nigga right now."

"No you won't." She flopped on the bed.

He turned around. "Fuck you talking about? If you think I'm letting this go you don't know me."

"I showed you for revenge but this video puts us both in a bind. You step to him and Denim is going to find out. Denim finds out and the same fate will reach me and I will be forced to leave. Now I'm okay with going at life on my own. Unlike Scarlett I got some cash saved up but you don't want that do you? I will rip this business apart from the outside."

"Race, I loved you and you fucked my brother?"

"And you fucked Scarlett." She paused rubbing her gut. "Consider us even."

"I will never forgive you for this."

"And what does that mean?"

He smiled at her and walked toward the door. Throwing her a sinister stare he said, "Don't worry, Race, your secret is safe with me. Believe that." He walked out the door.

What does that mean? She thought.

DENIM

Master was playing happily on Denim's bed when Bradley shuffled inside the room. She had cut her dreads and because of it her natural short mane retreated into tiny soft curls that complimented her face. She sliced her hair to symbolize letting her mother go because she was done being filled with regret for not being the daughter Sarah wanted. In her mind Sarah made a decision to leave and she would have to live with it, wherever she was in the world.

What she knew was this…she would not go looking for her, no matter what.

"Bambi said breakfast is ready," Bradley announced as he stuffed his hands into his black sweats, his dick print visible. "Hungry?"

"We're coming now." She kissed Master's forehead. "I just finished getting him dressed.

"You're doing good with him." Bradley smiled before picking Master up. "He seems really happy with you."

She looked back at him. "Thank you...he makes me happy. And you do too, Bradley."

He chuckled, uninterested in her in that way. "I got to admit, he's a cute little nigga. Head as big as my brother's but still cute."

"Thank you for letting me do this, Bradley. I know it's not your picture of what our family should be but I need to be a mother. More than I need anything else."

He kept his comment to himself believing she was also talking about their marriage. "I want to support your happiness, Denim," he handed her Master. "And you're right. This not my picture of what our life was meant to be but it's yours and I love you. So it means I'll have to deal with that." He winked. "I'm gonna help out in the kitchen. I'll see you in a minute."

On the way out the door he bumped into Race in the hallway who was rubbing her belly. The woman he really loved. Moving closer to her he said, "You okay?"

"I'm fine. A little stomachache that's all."

He nodded. "Well you look beautiful," he whispered. "And smell good, too."

"Don't do that," she begged. "Please don't do this to me."

"Race, I'm your friend, friends compliment each other don't they? Relax, I won't touch you again in that way, even if I think about you every night." He kissed her cheek and strolled away.

BAMBI

Bambi just finished putting the biscuits on the table. The weekly breakfast was her way of trying to repair her family but no one was sure if it was working. In her mind the only thing that was missing was Scarlett and as the months trailed by she realized how much she cared.

Still, she broke code and as a result had to be banished.

It took some time to get things back into relative ease. First they had to replenish the men Abd killed who moved their product and then they had to convince some of their customers that what happened to the rival gangs would not happen to them. Some bought it but others didn't which meant a fifteen percent decrease in profit as those folk sought other Plugs.

Then there was the pain of what losing Sarge meant. Emotionally and professionally his absence meant they had to be more on hand with the product than they preferred. The Mexican distributors still packaged the work and made the deliveries, still believing Mitch was alive of course, but they were growing suspicious since they now had to speak to Kevin instead of Sarge who'd been one on one with them in the past.

Luckily Kevin had a bond with Mitch before he was murdered and it was easier to see how he would be chosen by the Mexican officials. Still, Suarez Vidal was starting to grow weary of not being able to talk to Mitch and planned a trip next week to visit America, which the Kennedy's did not know about.

Definitely another trial was coming the Kennedy's way.

Bambi was scooping eggs on the plate when Kevin walked up to her and watched her breakfast flow. "Yvette and Carissa called again. Did you tell them we aren't selling to them anymore?"

Bambi sighed. "Let me deal with Yvette and Carissa from now on, Kevin. Don't worry, I have them under control."

He wiped his hand down his face. "Well, Melo coming home tomorrow from college."

"I know. I talked to him. He never comes home on breaks. I guess all the men we have guarding him is making him uncomfortable."

"It's the nature of the lifestyle we lead." He looked at the Mimosa she was nursing in the champagne flute. "So you have no intentions on stopping this shit? You gonna sip your way into each hour, refusing to deal with life?"

"I like a little drink every now and then." She shrugged. "So what. You yourself said I cut back a lot, Kevin. So lets not make this harder than it should be by getting on my nerves while I'm cooking."

"So you won't even try to get help? For me?"

"Did you get help when you fucked Believe? Or the young bitch?" She paused. "Is that what your idea of help was? Fucking two bad bitches at the same time?" she giggled. "Nigga, please. Get the fuck out of my face before I slice your throat and your dick."

Kevin backed away and he wanted to shit on himself. "Who...who told you that?"

"She called me a few days after I put them out but I knew already. I thought about it when I was sober. It was in the way she looked at me when she called herself telling me off. A woman knows when another woman has had her man. It doesn't take rocket science.

But I will tell you this, neither one of them bitches better not be pregnant. Or you gonna see a monster, Mr. Kennedy." She took a sip of Mimosa. "Now put the forks on the table and stop fucking with me, Kevin. Before I toss this family upside down. And we both know I'm fully capable."

He cleared his throat and left her alone.

One by one the Kennedy's piled inside the kitchen and had a lovely breakfast. Well, all except Ramirez. He was still salty as fuck.

The others put aside the secrets of betrayal, lust and love.

For the moment anyway.

SCARLETT

Scarlett sat on the park bench biting her nails. Living on her own had not been good for her, which is why she welcomed the surprise call she received earlier in the day. She couldn't go to the Kennedy compound because she fucked Ramirez and she couldn't go to her white family because she married a black man.

Essentially she was alone and needed help.

Desperately.

When she saw Race walking in the park pushing a designer black buggy with Master inside she held her trembling lips as they approached. She never realized how much she missed both of them until that moment.

Standing in front of Race she said, "Can I hug you?"

Race sighed and extended her palm. "Not yet, Scarlett. Not yet."

"I respect that and understand." She looked down at Master. "Can I...pick him up?"

"Of course...He's your baby and he needs you."

Slowly Scarlett lowered her body and raised up her child. He was happier than she remembered him and didn't cry like he had in the past. "I can tell he's being loved. Thank you for this...so much."

"We gonna look after him, Scarlett. You know that. Blood born Kennedy's are the only ones safe for true love."

"Thank you."

"Why, Scarlett?" Race asked. "Why did you do it?"

Scarlett placed Master in the carriage and sat down on the wooden bench. Race flopped next to her and waited for the answer. "Loneliness has a way of

Pretty Kings 4: Race's Rage

temporarily blinding you, Race. Making you feel like any attention you get in the moment is all that matters. Not making excuses but you can't see the consequences for your actions nor do you want to. It's like a drug and I was wrong."

Race sighed. "You hurt me but I love you."

"I love you too, Race and I'm so sorry. For everything."

Race looked out into the park. "Where you been staying?"

"Wherever I can. I've had to do some pretty bad things since the family has cut me off but I gotta own my own shit. Not complaining at all. Trust me."

Race nodded. "I understand why you did what you did. Sometimes you get caught up in the moment like you said. Shit happens." She sighed. "I forgive you and I want you to know I'm telling the family to let you back into the compound."

Scarlett's brows rose. "Are you serious?"

"I wouldn't play like this." She paused. "We have a sick dynamic in our family. In the heat of the moment we kill, lie and do what we need to but when it comes to family we still love each other. And, Scarlett, you are family."

"You're right. Look at what you're doing now. You didn't have to come visit me but you did. I mean, Denim and Bambi call me all the time but you came and gave me some money because you care."

Race laughed. "I knew it! They tried to act like they didn't know what you were up to. I had a feeling they were connecting with you though."

"All I want to do is come home. Can I? Please."

"Take this for now." Race dug into her purse and handed her ten thousand dollars. "I'm definitely gonna talk to the fam. But I need to know if you do come back that I can trust you."

"You can trust me, Race. And I'm done with Ramirez. Sister's before misters."

Race laughed. "Corny but I like it." She ran her hand down the side of Scarlett's beautiful face. "But first…"

Race rose up. "First what?"

"I have to make a few alterations."

Scarlett giggled. "What you talking about, Race?"

"Like I said, I have to change some things up before letting you back in the home."

Scarlett was so focused on Race's expression that she didn't see the five women from the hood she hired walking behind her. When she finally turned around

276   **Pretty Kings 4:** Race's Rage

and saw them she grew scared. Now she knew what was up. Race was still on her rage shit. "Race....don't do this...I'm begging you."

"When I first thought about how I could get back at you I told myself our family meant more to you than anything. So I decided to take that from you. But it turns out that was only half the truth. You see...you love us, no doubt. But what you really love is your beauty. It has allowed you into places that most can't go. So I must take it from you first. If you want, after taking this beat down, you can come home but you'll never look the same."

"You don't have to do this, Race."

"Beat her ass!" Race ordered. "Paying special attention to that face. I want it real fucked up."

Pushing the carriage with one hand, Race walked away, Scarlett's screams behind her. She almost reached her car when her phone rang from an unknown number. "Who is this?" She stopped.

"Race..." the caller said.

She realized it was the voice of her New Friend and froze in place. "Why are you calling me? All of a sudden?"

"It ain't about us," he said. "Someone wants to talk to you."

"Hello, Race Kennedy?" Roman's voice came on the line.

"How do you know...how...my friend?"

"It was all a set up, Race. The job where you were hired for the movie company, getting you to reveal your secrets. Everything. The man you were talking to was Owen. A very good friend of mine."

"But why do all of this?"

"Because you killed my friend Carey."

"But...what...what are you talking about?" Race said frantically. "I loved Carey. I told you that. She was close to me."

"Is that why you fucked her and killed her?"

"Whoever gave you this information is wrong!"

"There's no need in lying. Sarah, Denim's mother, told me a long time ago. And I held it back until this contract was over. But it's done now right?"

Race felt dizzy. The last person she needed on her trail was Roman. "So what now?"

"Say your goodbyes. Before I murder you I'm going to ruin your world. Your friends don't know half of the secrets you told Owen about them but I know them all and soon they will too. Rest up, Race Kennedy. You're going to need it before your world collapses."

When the call was over the first thing that came to Race's mind was KARMA.

The Cartel Publications Order Form

www.thecartelpublications.com

Inmates **ONLY** receive novels for $10.00 per book.

(Mail Order **MUST** come from inmate directly to receive discount)

Shyt List 1	_____	$15.00
Shyt List 2	_____	$15.00
Shyt List 3	_____	$15.00
Shyt List 4	_____	$15.00
Shyt List 5	_____	$15.00
Pitbulls In A Skirt	_____	$15.00
Pitbulls In A Skirt 2	_____	$15.00
Pitbulls In A Skirt 3	_____	$15.00
Pitbulls In A Skirt 4	_____	$15.00
Pitbulls In A Skirt 5	_____	$15.00
Victoria's Secret	_____	$15.00
Poison 1	_____	$15.00
Poison 2	_____	$15.00
Hell Razor Honeys	_____	$15.00
Hell Razor Honeys 2	_____	$15.00
A Hustler's Son	_____	$15.00
A Hustler's Son 2	_____	$15.00
Black and Ugly	_____	$15.00
Black and Ugly As Ever	_____	$15.00
Year Of The Crackmom	_____	$15.00
Deadheads	_____	$15.00
The Face That Launched A	_____	$15.00
Thousand Bullets		
The Unusual Suspects	_____	$15.00
Miss Wayne & The Queens of DC	_____	$15.00
Paid In Blood (eBook Only)	_____	$15.00
Raunchy	_____	$15.00
Raunchy 2	_____	$15.00
Raunchy 3	_____	$15.00
Mad Maxxx	_____	$15.00
Quita's Dayscare Center	_____	$15.00
Quita's Dayscare Center 2	_____	$15.00
Pretty Kings	_____	$15.00
Pretty Kings 2	_____	$15.00
Pretty Kings 3	_____	$15.00
Pretty Kings 4	_____	$15.00
Silence Of The Nine	_____	$15.00
Silence Of The Nine 2	_____	$15.00
Prison Throne	_____	$15.00
Drunk & Hot Girls	_____	$15.00
Hersband Material	_____	$15.00
The End: How To Write A	_____	$15.00
Bestselling Novel In 30 Days (Non-Fiction Guide)		
Upscale Kittens	_____	$15.00
Wake & Bake Boys	_____	$15.00
Young & Dumb	_____	$15.00
Young & Dumb 2:	_____	$15.00
Tranny 911	_____	$15.00
Tranny 911: Dixie's Rise	_____	$15.00

Pretty Kings 4: Race's Rage

First Comes Love, Then Comes Murder _____		$15.00
Luxury Tax _____		$15.00
The Lying King _____		$15.00
Crazy Kind Of Love _____		$15.00
And They Call Me God _____		$15.00
The Ungrateful Bastards _____		$15.00
Lipstick Dom _____		$15.00
A School of Dolls _____		$15.00
Hoetic Justice _____		$15.00
KALI: Raunchy Relived _____		$15.00
Skeezers _____		$15.00
You Kissed Me, Now I Own You _____		$15.00
Nefarious _____		$15.00
Redbone 3: The Rise of The Fold _____		$15.00
Clown Niggas _____		$15.00

(**Redbone 1** & **2** are **NOT** Cartel Publications novels and if **ordered** the cost is **FULL** price of $15.00 **each. No Exceptions**.)

Please add $5.00 **PER BOOK** for shipping and handling.

The Cartel Publications * P.O. BOX 486 OWINGS MILLS MD 21117

Name: _____

Address: _____

City/State: _____

Contact/Email: _____

Please allow 5-7 BUSINESS days before shipping.

The Cartel Publications is NOT responsible for Prison Orders rejected, NO RETURNS and NO REFUNDS.

NO PERSONAL CHECKS ACCEPTED

STAMPS NO LONGER ACCEPTED

By **T. Styles**   281

CPSIA information can be obtained
at www.ICGtesting.com
Printed in the USA
LVOW12s1536100117
520452LV00002B/313/P